BY

ÉLIETTE ABÉCASSIS

If Only

BY

ÉLIETTE ABÉCASSIS

If Only

TRANSLATED FROM THE FRENCH
BY JOHANNA MCCALMONT

W1-Media, Inc.
Grand Books
Stamford, CT, USA

Copyright © 2023 by W1-Media Inc. for this edition
© Éditions Grasset & Fasquelle, 2020
First hardcover English edition published by W1-Media Inc. /
Grand Books 2023

Visit our website at www.arctis-books.com

1 3 5 7 9 8 6 4 2

The Library of Congress Control Number: 2023930113
ISBN 978-1-64690-038-1
eBook ISBN 978-1-64690-627-7
English translation copyright © Johanna McCalmont, 2023

Excerpt on page 13 translated by A.S. Kline, 2021.
From Letter VII
Used with permission by Poetry in Translation

Printed in China

To Ilan, my first rendez-vous

1.

A long hallway, Paris, the Sorbonne University, eye contact. There they were, nothing out of the ordinary, standing in the same line outside the secretary's office. Just two people chatting, making small talk—the kind of interaction that happens countless times in life.

With her dark clothes, bangs, glasses, and a dash of kohl under her eyes, she was the vision of someone who had just emerged from adolescence when she came up the stairs from the first floor with her best friend Clara—who was dressed in red and black and half hidden under a hat twice the size of her head—and three other classmates. All students at the Sorbonne, the small group shared the same outlook on life and a large apartment with several other roommates, including a young man who spoke a language they had yet to identify—Greek, Croatian, or Swiss German perhaps—and who had been living with them for months without anyone really knowing where he'd come from or what he was in fact doing there. Their home in the heart of the Latin Quarter was a sort of squat, but it's where they held suitably boozy parties, and where, at night, the empty bones of chicken cadavers and half-empty bottles—or possibly the reverse—lay strewn alongside each other. The five students had met while campaigning for the anti-racism NGO SOS Racisme. They had been protesting about the death of Malik Oussekine—killed during the protests against the Devaquet Law that aimed to reform higher education—and that evening they had ended up together, handing out leaflets and fighting, albeit not entirely sure what for, other than the need to quench their thirst for political activism.

With his jacket, white shirt, round glasses, and curly hair, he was a bit of a catch, a bit Parisian, and he had come from Saint-Germain to sign up for economics. He was polite, shy, socialist, and had welcomed Mitterrand's election. He was with his friend Charles: a serious-looking Corsican with a frown and a knowing smile. The pair had met in a lecture and campaigned against the far right together.

After registration, they all headed to Place de la Sorbonne for a coffee together. The conversation continued, about this and that, about dreams. The young man and young woman eventually introduced themselves to each other. Her name was Amélie, his was Vincent. Her family was from Normandy; she was studying literature and planned to go into teaching. She had brown hair, dark rings under her eyes that looked at the world as though surprised to discover it in color, a delicate frame, a slim silhouette, and a shy smile; still a child, barely a woman. She wondered if he'd give her his phone number, if he'd want to call her, if he liked her as much as she liked him. If it was better to show how she felt, or hide it, or simply say nothing at all. If she was pretty enough, or if she had some kind of flaw that was a turn-off, something about her he didn't like. Was her nose too big, were her cheekbones too prominent, was her haircut terrible, did she lack that feminine allure? She was impressed by the way he spoke, the strand of hair that fell over his eyes, his handsome face, the intensity of his expression, his warm voice—deep yet soft, refined. His character was strong yet gentle, and he was polite and seemed to have been brought up well, a little distant but pleasant. There was a hint of creativity, like a mild madness. Sometimes he seemed to be elsewhere, a dilettante, a dreamer. He was musical, and playing piano was the thing he enjoyed most.

Later, the group walked through Paris like tourists. They crossed the bridge, went to the Île Saint-Louis, admired the Seine at sunset, sat on the riverbanks, and talked about their lives. Vincent, sitting in the middle of the group, was fascinated. Seeing her like that, opposite him, so strange, shy, and captivating; she seemed both innocent and impish at the same time. He told himself he had met someone interesting, profound, cultivated—someone who seemed to understand him, to whom he would be able to talk. She was both charming and odd, a little sad, like she was lost in the city. Could she be interested in someone like him? She seemed unapproachable. Yet there she was, beside him, and they were chatting.

Dressed in dark clothes and uncomfortable in her own skin no matter what she wore, what she did, or what she said, her shyness and negative self-image often made her express herself in a way that was slightly confusing. Her mother had repeatedly told her, "With looks like yours, my dear, you'll have to make up for them with intelligence." Perhaps she intrigued him? She didn't dare believe it. He was attractive and had a scar on his left cheek, a bit like that guy Robert Hossein in *Angélique*, cloaked in cologne and surrounded by girls! There was a slight aloofness about him, and he had a way of looking at her that stopped her in her tracks. Charm oozed from his eyes, and in his deep, almost gentle voice, he asked her what she did. She began to stutter, said she studied, tutored to earn money, wrote in her spare time, liked art, painting, sculpture, went running in the Jardin du Luxembourg with her Walkman. And what about him, was he from Paris? Yes, Montmartre, the hill with the vines, a large apartment, parents who ran a store and didn't understand him at all or his passion: music. As a child, he had had a teacher—a neighbor who taught at the conservatory in the 17th arrondissement—who had lit his passion for the piano.

Amélie had had a rigorous provincial upbringing and led an ordered life. Her school principal father had never let her go out as a teenager. She had never been allowed to go to bars or parties, which her parents called "blasts"—a word from the teenybopper 1960s they hadn't really experienced themselves—or invite friends of the opposite sex over. She may have been born in 1968, but it felt like the women's liberation movement hadn't happened where she had grown up, or even come anywhere near her family home. She had read Simone de Beauvoir, who had become her role model, her ideal, and had sworn to herself that, one day, she would exist in her own right. She took refuge in books, to see herself reflected, to flee reality.

The weather that evening was beautiful, and the city was already sluggishly succumbing to that summer feeling. People strolled along the banks of the river, past the cafes. Old people, young people, children, women, men, lovers. Couples sat on benches. The streets toward the Marais with its bakeries and restaurants selling falafel and shawarma on the streetside were a joyful hustle and bustle.

When the others decided to go home, he suggested going for a coffee. Why not? They had time. They continued chatting as they crossed the bridge, walked around some more, stopped at a stall selling books on the banks of the Seine. For just a few coins, you could pick up romance novels, thrillers, potboilers, sappy novels, stories within stories, stories that were exciting, new, old, futuristic, manuals, essays, books about psychology or philosophy, history books or story books, and even poetry anthologies.

It was a time when people read: in the metro, in the street, at the beach, in bed, in the bath, in the kitchen.

People brought books to parks, gardens, swimming pools, waiting rooms, on buses, trains, and planes. They read in armchairs, on sofas, in living rooms, in hotels, in cafés and bars, in towns and villages, in the summer and winter, in the evening and the morning, while eating, before bed, when they got up, with a cup of tea or a glass of wine, beside the fire as the day came to an end. People read everywhere, at any time of the day, at any time of life, to read another story, escape reality or experience it more intensely, understand others, hate them, or simply pass the time. Every Friday evening, Amélie would watch *Apostrophes* on TV and listen to Bernard Pivot interview authors with a passion. Roland Barthes, Françoise Sagan, Albert Cohen, Truffaut, Jankélévitch, Le Roy Ladurie or Duby, all of them wearing ties, apart from Bernard-Henri Lévi. Vincent preferred Michel Polac who, sitting in a cloud of smoke, would comment on the debates around the magazines *Charlie Hebdo*, *Minute*, and *Hara-Kiri*, while Serge Gainsbourg—wearing his signature sunglasses—would say "shit'" and Pierre Desproges would expound upon athletes' intelligence to Guy Drut.

The two students talked for a while about what they enjoyed reading, asking each other if they knew various writers. They both found and bought something to their taste. Amélie picked a first edition of *Belle du Seigneur*, and Vincent chose *Rilke's Letters to a Young Poet*. She selected hers for the notion that passion is not real love, for the setting in a villa in the south of France where the lovers get bored after having loved each other like crazy.

He chose his for the text: "And so loving is, for a long time to come and far into life—solitude, a growing and deepening solitude for those who love." Then they looked at each other. It was time to say goodbye. So he suggested going for a beer on Quai des Grands-Augustins. The drink turned into dinner, and when they decided to go for another beer, everywhere in the city had already closed because it was so late. So they walked to Café des Capucines, on the boulevard with the same name, open all night. And they talked a while longer. About themselves. About their parents, their desires, their hopes, their friends. About the films they liked, *Out of Africa*, *Marathon Man*, *Barry Lindon*. And about music, the Beatles, Queen, and Chopin.

It got even later, and drinks turned into coffees as they shared a few secrets. How his father had hit him when he was a child, right up to the day he had outgrown him by a head and threatened his father in turn. How her parents fought all the time, going as far as throwing plates at each other, yet wouldn't separate. How they had both been raised with the sole purpose of pleasing their parents, following the laws laid down by their fathers. But she had only one dream: to seize her freedom and become independent. He toed the line because his father still supported him, which meant he could study without having to work. After midnight, he told her about his brother, his older brother who was twenty-seven and sick. She knew a few people who had AIDS as well, and a friend of a friend was waiting for test results because his partner had told him she had gotten it too.

"Do you spend a lot of time caring for him?" she asked.

"I visit him at the hospital every day. It's intense, exhausting."

"What does he talk about?" she asked.

"He tells me about his life. The secret one my parents don't know about. He tells me everything. He talks about all sorts of things we never talked about before he got sick. We've never been as close, and I've somehow realized I never really knew him before."

"It must be hard," she said.

"I do what I can to help him."

"Do you have any other brothers and sisters?" she asked.

"No. There are just the two of us," he replied.

"So he's only got you?"

"He's got a lot of friends who are around, thankfully. What about you?"

"There are three of us. I'm the middle one," she said.

"A tricky position."

"Yes, I struggle to find my place. I feel like I'm an extra. The ugly duckling. That's what my mother says."

"What does she say?" he asked.

"That I'm not pretty."

"You are pretty," he told her.

"Really?" she asked.

"Yes," he said, looking into her eyes as they sat opposite each other, hands resting on the mahogany table in an art nouveau style café that had been flamboyantly decorated in bright colors with red seats, crimson-colored lamps, and a *Belle Epoque* skylight in the ceiling above them. Behind the large windows framed by curtains, the boulevard outside was empty. Something akin to silence had settled around them. In that moment, he could have taken her hand, just her hand, or perhaps held her face, and given her a kiss, or simply touched her cheek, and waited. She could have smiled at him, held his gaze instead of lowering her eyes modestly. She had thought about getting up and sitting beside him. He could have simply put his arm around her; she would have nestled her head against his neck. Or they could have kissed, and everything would have changed with just one sentence, or a word, *that* word, "yes." But, voluntarily or not, out of thoughtfulness or fear, pride or prejudice, recklessness, or the awareness that one gesture, a simple gesture would be irreversible, the silence continued, then had to be broken.

"If you had the choice today, what would you most like to do?" she asked.

"Play piano," he replied.

"So why did you sign up for a degree in economics?"

"My father doesn't want me to become a musician. There's only one piano in an orchestra—it wouldn't lead anywhere."

"Are you good?" she asked.

"I went to the conservatory in my neighborhood, in Montmartre."

"So you could have kept it up and studied music?"

"Yes, maybe. But not as far as my father was concerned," he said.

"You sound like you're afraid of him?"

"Well, I used to be, yes . . . but I'm not afraid of him now, not in the slightest. And what about you? What are you afraid of?" he asked her.

"Y2K. Aren't you?"

"No, why would I? It's just hype."

"It's the end of the millennium. I'm worried about it. No one knows what lies ahead. It feels like it's the end of a world."

"All the better," he said. "I like change. It's exciting, not knowing."

"When I was in Bernay, there was only one thing I couldn't wait for: getting to Paris."

"Do you like Paris?" he asked.

"I love it. I can finally breathe here. I was suffocating in Bernay. I know what life outside Paris is like. We used to organize meetings and protests all over the place with SOS," she continued.

"I was at the high school student demo when they killed Malik Oussekine," he said.

"So was I! We could have met. Are you still involved in politics?"

"I'm a member of the socialist party."

"Why?" she asked.

"Why not? In his memoirs, François Mitterrand says that life is like judo. One day you're down, and then, in a single move, you can turn it all around and end up on top. That's politics," he explained.

"But life's not like that."

"It isn't? What is it like then?" he asked.

16

"I think everything changes and we don't even notice. We get caught up in the things around us—they overpower us and eventually end up controlling us. And we don't have much room for maneuvering," she said.

"Have you ever been in love?" he asked her.

"Yes. With my philosophy teacher! I hung on his every last word. He was the one who made me want to study literature at university. What about you?"

"I met an older woman when I was sixteen."

"How old was she?"

"She's forty now."

"That's a huge age gap. Did you break up?"

"We knew it wouldn't last."

"Was she a pianist?"

"How did you guess?" he asked.

"It's . . . logical. You shared the same passion," she replied.

"You know, it's strange, I don't know you. I've never told anyone this. She was my piano teacher at the conservatory. My father did everything he could to get me to leave her."

"And you left her because of him?"

"Yes. It was a dangerous game for her too," he added.

"Was she married?" she asked.

"Yes, and she has children."

"So it was love," she concluded.

"You believe in love?"

"Yes, of course."

"True love?"

"That too. And you?"

"I don't know. How old are you?" he asked.

They were twenty years old. Only twenty. And it was as they left the Café des Capucines, just as dawn was breaking, that their relationship should have begun. They should have met again, gone for a drink, then another, been attracted to each other, admitted that they were, and then kissed on the banks of the Seine as they left the cinema, or a restaurant, called each other to say the most trivial thing, and then, one evening, or night, or perhaps at dawn as the day began, after a thousand embraces and a thousand kisses, made love and fell in love, loved each other and said it, said it and gotten married, after a few days, a few months, or a few years, at the town hall in Bernay or Montmartre, in the presence of their respective, respectful families, a white dress and a bouquet of flowers, and perhaps a child, or two, or three, watched their first smiles, their first words, their first steps, taken photos and made photo albums, went on vacation to the seaside and built sandcastles, taken young children to the playground, then to school, celebrated birthdays, watched them grow up, leave home, start university one day, at the Sorbonne, where they had met, where they still liked to recall their youth and that day standing in line in that hallway, when their eyes met, along with their destinies.

But none of that happened, none of that happened at all.

2.

Vincent quickened his pace so he wouldn't be late. He was always extremely punctual, generally early rather than late. He arrived at the café on Place de la Sorbonne, reached into his pocket, and brought out what remained of the old watch with the broken face that he treasured. A watch his great-grandfather had given to his grandfather, who had given it to his father, who, in turn, had given it to him on his first communion. His grandfather had also given him his passion for music and the piano. He had insisted on sending him to the conservatory because he thought his grandson was talented, much to the chagrin of his own son. A music-loving grandfather who loved playing piano. Vincent kept that watch on him at all times, like a talisman, to mark the time that passed.

He was ten minutes early. He didn't want to miss this date. He had liked her. She had a certain *je ne sais quoi*. A young man began to play the violin on the square—a captivating air by Fauré—and Vincent's mind began to meander back through his teenage years. He remembered his neighbor, a concert pianist who had taught him everything he knew. How he had entered the conservatory where he attended music theory, piano, and singing lessons. The exams, competitions, relentless work how he had repeated a single bar 1,500 times to achieve perfection because not the slightest error was permitted. The final diploma and first prize. Words of encouragement from everyone, apart from his father.

He would have given up everything. His city, his life, his soul, his heart. He would have devoted himself entirely. Day and night, morning, and evening. Dedicated his body and soul, offered himself up. When he was immersed, nothing else mattered at all; his cares disappeared without a trace. His father, a tyrant, his mother, submissive and self-effacing, resigned, almost defeated. Instead of running away, escaping or fleeing, he had found comfort in his passion. But it had been demanding, didn't give itself up easily. Each day, each hour, each minute had to be conquered. It had to be earned, was evasive, transformed to escape his grasp, demanded exclusivity, couldn't stand the slightest competition or flaw, and, above all, demanded that one sacrificed one's life. It was the thing he loved above everything else: music. He had wanted to devote himself to his art, but his father had not given him the choice. *Do you know how many pianists there are in an orchestra? Music is a hobby. You need a profession, a real one.* So, he had agreed to choose a "real" subject, to make his parents proud and happy following the tragedy that had struck his family with his brother's illness.

He sat there alone for a moment, reflecting. Vincent. Vincent Brunel. He would have liked to have changed his name, if only the process hadn't been so complicated. A name determines you, takes hold of you. His made him sound like a manager, a perfect little soldier. But he didn't recognize himself at all in that description. He planned to travel, dreamed of being somewhere else. Paris wasn't enough for him. He had crisscrossed the city, back and forth, knew every last cobblestone. Whenever he left, he loved returning and rediscovering it from a different perspective, but he wanted to leave for good, for the other side of the world. Impossible, of course, given the circumstances. He glanced at his watch again. 5:05 p.m. What on earth could she be doing? He didn't like tardiness.

This girl, Amélie. He had never spent as much time with anyone else, talking until dawn, about anything and everything. He wanted to continue their conversation. She was special, the way she listened to him, lowering her head slightly, as though to hear him better. He'd told her everything about his life, even his first love, that passionate teen love, but he didn't know much about her. She was reserved, discrete, astute. Even shier than he was. He should have taken her hand that evening. They had parted ways without a word, too quickly. He hadn't dared to. When he had arrived home, he had opened the book she'd given him and been surprised to find her name there, Amélie, along with her phone number. He smiled. He'd had the same idea; she should have found his number on the flyleaf of the Rilke. He had called her, set up this date, and she had said yes, 5 o'clock. At the café on Place de la Sorbonne. Had she got the time wrong? Had they misunderstood each other? He got up, walked around a bit to relax, make sure he didn't look upset, and was struck, suddenly overwhelmed, in fact, by the thought she wouldn't come. He listened to the music; the violinist was good and had just started a spellbinding sonata by Fauré, "After a dream."

There he was, alone, waiting for a girl who wasn't going to show up. Perhaps she had forgotten? Perhaps they hadn't even arranged a date? Perhaps it had all been a dream? But there was the phone number, and the book. He made his way to a phone booth, got a few coins out, and called her. He waited for at least ten rings, then hung up. She probably wasn't interested in him. People often told him he was cold. There was indeed something distant about him that made others feel uncomfortable. Was this perhaps a date with himself? Should he insist, call again, or leave?

After a while—almost an hour—he gave up hope. He got up from the bench and slowly walked away. He disappeared around the corner into Boulevard Saint-Michel just as a girl in a black dress, exhausted and out of breath, arrived on the square. The square was full of surprises and sudden twists—a cruel, savage theater of life governed by a plot that remains a mystery, always more troubling than any novel because reality is never credible, just as Amélie had written in her final high-school French exam in response to that well-known quote from Guy de Maupassant's preface to *Pierre et Jean*. As she arrived, Vincent was already disappearing into the distance, at a brisk pace. Disappointed, but not disheartened. He was leaving with friends the next day for a trip around Europe by train and bicycle. A vacation that had been carefully planned for months: Switzerland, Italy, Greece . . . as far as Egypt! No, honestly, none of this was of any great importance.

3.

An old gray telephone with a handset and rotary dial that clicked as a call was placed. The first few numbers were easy to dial, but the last ones took longer. You had to be careful you didn't make a mistake, otherwise you had to start again. And each time it rang loudly, you would run to answer it.

Amélie had one of those phones beside her bed in the room in the apartment she shared with her countless roommates. Everyone had their own because there was nothing more tiring than standing in the hallway during those hour-long conversations with the receiver tucked between your ear and shoulder.

She had hesitated one second too long before answering the phone. What if it was her mother? Or Vincent? Wanting to cancel . . . She wanted to see him so much that she didn't want to run that risk.

Entangled, embroiled, ensnared in her own malaise, she simply couldn't get up. Lying prostrate on her bed, as though paralyzed, she couldn't even stretch out her hand to pick up the phone. Something irrepressible prevented her, like a force weighing her down, catching her around her neck, trapping her. Like an iron hand gripping her while a voice whispered, *You shall not leave this room. You shall not live your life as a woman. You shall only find fulfillment through work and sacrifice. You shall not know the joy of loving and being loved.* She wanted to tear herself free, but it was stronger than her, stronger than anything else. Like chains tying her to her bed.

She could see the rooftops of Paris from her room. Sloping slate roofs, shades of gray; she liked to contemplate the rooftops shining in the summer sun. She was happy she was there, that she had arrived safe and sound, even though life was hard, the people harsh, and the sky often gray. Paris seduced her and scared her: she had dreamt of it the first time her parents had taken her there. A trip to the capital was unbelievably exciting for a twelve-year-old! They had visited Beaubourg and the Louvre and wandered down the banks of the Seine, passing the book stalls. And she had sensed that this city was her city, that she felt good there, and that, one day, she would live there. A bed, a desk, posters of Robert Doisneau and Gustav Klimt's famous *Kiss* painting, and a shared bathroom. She could fend for herself. In periods of scarcity, she didn't eat anything, counted every last penny, and kept studying. She was gifted with a vital instinct that helped her overcome obstacles; she had managed to leave her city, her life, and sign up for a literature degree in Paris. When she had lived in Bernay, everyone in the small town had known her every last move. She had only been allowed out to run errands if they needed something from the grocery store across the road. When she had been younger, her father would call ahead whenever she went to a friend's house to make sure she had indeed arranged to meet them. Her every move had been monitored when she had been in high school. She had basically lived under the Reign of Terror, the 1986 version. Her only refuge had been books and music. Those were the days of Barbra Streisand's "Woman in love," the Scorpions' "Still loving you," and Gilbert Montagné's *"On va s'aimer."* The days of the first headphones, cassette recordings from the radio, VHS films, and roller skates with two wheels at the front and two at the back. The days of *Fame, Flashdance*, and *Dirty Dancing*. When *Charlie's Angels* and *Starsky and Hutch* or *Magnum* were the Sunday highlight and everyone was in love with Anne Sinclair who hosted the Sunday evening politics show. Those were the days of house parties and concerts, the film *The Party*, and shivers down your spine while watching the outrageous *9 ½ Weeks*.

The phone stopped ringing. She heard footsteps—it was Clara. Her roommate knocked on the door and came in. She was wearing a jogging suit and was tailed by a dog that started to charge around the room like a mad thing, buzzing with excitement.

"Are you coming? We're going out for a run," said Clara.

"I've got a date," replied Amélie.

"Who with?"

"That guy I met, remember? At university, the other day."

"Awesome! Well, what are you waiting for? It's the first date you've had since you got here," said Clara.

"I don't know what to wear."

"Do you want to borrow my red dress?" Clara suggested.

Amélie pictured herself in Clara's amazing dress: long, figure-hugging, low-cut, and disconnected from reality, her reality as a student who felt uncomfortable in her own skin.

"No. I'll wear jeans. I'm late," said Amélie.

"Get going then, hurry up."

With Clara's encouragement, she managed to get up and pull on a pair of pants and a T-shirt. Then she changed her mind and slipped into a flowery summer dress, looked at her reflection, delayed her departure by trying on a flared skirt and a little flowery top, and finally left the apartment in a black dress. As soon as she stepped out onto the sidewalk, everything around her started to spin. An imaginary whirlwind made her feel dizzy, and anxiety tightened her throat. She started to run for her life, racing up Boulevard Saint-Michel, zigzagging between other pedestrians, trying to make up for the time she had lost. But she was too late. The square was busy, but Vincent wasn't there. She sat down on a bench beside a violinist, and in a dreamy melancholy, listened to the music, not realizing she would have to wait at least ten years to see Vincent again.

4.

It was 10:30 p. m. on December 31ˢᵗ of that fateful year, 1999. In a smoky apartment in the Bastille neighborhood, an eclectic mix of partygoers talked over a trip-hop soundtrack. The host, a trendy young writer, was smoking weed, like most of the guests. There was a desire to be done with the millennium, with the old world. The plastic cups, bottles of whiskey, and potato chips on paper tablecloths were all a reminder of their student days. As they listened to Louise Attaque and Massive Attack, a few guests seriously attacked the bottle of whiskey doing the rounds. With women wearing barely any makeup, guys in shirts and jeans, editors, musicians, and a few actors, the eclectic crowd partied, looking somewhat miserable, not happy in the slightest, like they had to, like it was an obligation or they were on automatic pilot, not really knowing what to do because it was such an extraordinary occasion, one that only happened once in a thousand years.

Amélie taught literature in a Paris lycée, lived in a small studio apartment on the top floor of an apartment building without an elevator on Montagne Sainte-Geneviève, and visited her parents less and less often. She had freed herself of the ballast of her upbringing, and returning to her childhood home only gave her panic attacks. Each time she arrived in Bernay station, it felt like she had stepped back into the past. She only ever stayed a few days, just long enough to visit her parents who were alone now that her sisters had gone, one to New York and the other off the rails.

She had come to the party reluctantly, dragged there by her best friend Clara in an extremely old, bashed up, white Fiat full of all manner of objects, clothes, memories, and a huge dog her friend had found howling at the moon in the road one night and ended up adopting because her other dog had recently died. The stray would bark wildly whenever Clara left, no doubt afraid it was being abandoned again, so she had to take it with her everywhere.

They had both donned hats and black dresses, along with round sunglasses, a fad of Clara's because she currently had a thing for the sixties. Amélie had changed her style. Brown hair, light-colored eyes, and a smile that was a little reserved. She was slimmer now, looked taller in heels, and had let her bangs grow out, but she had kept her long hair and childlike smile. She felt slightly awkward as she arrived, shy and apprehensive, like a child still cowering behind the young woman. A boy had once told her that her hair looked horrible in front of the rest of their classmates. She had turned scarlet, ashamed, and awkward. Those sorts of scars from adolescence leave a mark. They last a lifetime, like a hot iron, creating the fear deep down that you're ridiculous, that you're not wearing the right clothes, that you don't fit in, that you look stupid . . . They created that girl who felt uncomfortable in her own skin, who didn't dare go to parties, who wasn't invited, who didn't know how to dance, and who stayed in the corner, hiding behind the likable face of the young woman she was trying to project. And yet, at the age of thirty, she was on her own, looking at the other guests, wondering who she could talk to. She had been in a relationship with an uncommunicative guy for three years, who was another student in her course who she had met in a lecture. She had struggled to leave him because she had been afraid of ending up alone, scared she'd never meet her soulmate even though she wanted to experience a passionate relationship, like in the books she continued to buy on the banks of the Seine, out of habit, out of weariness, out of a melancholic notion of romance, out of the desire to marry and have children.

When she finally managed to extricate herself from that relationship, she had wandered from smile to smile, arm to arm, day to day, looking for love more than affairs, desire more than pleasure, feelings more than wants, and dreams more than passion. She was an anti-conformist who didn't like following rules, who hated the middle class and the adoption of middle-class values. She was completely dispossessed of everything material, professed to be a spendthrift, didn't want to own anything and didn't own anything—no furniture, no jewelry, no knickknacks. She would barely eat for an entire week, consuming only vegetables, she didn't follow fashion trends and distanced herself from all social obligations. She would have liked to have been as light as a bird, perched on a branch, or higher in the sky, where the body does not exist, only the soul, soaring up and away, only seeing the earth's infinite beauty, up there where only magnificence, splendor, calm, and delight exist.

Clara, on the other hand, had already identified her prey: a young man around thirty like her who looked like an actor and, in fact, was. She had swooped in on him, asking if he knew the host well. It was a run-of-the-mill opening line, but effective. They were now chatting, laughing, and drinking while Amélie stood there on her own, but she wasn't okay on her own. She had a drink, then another; she liked feeling a little tipsy. She took a drag on a joint that was doing the rounds, and then, in the middle of all the other guests, she saw him: the young man she had met at the Sorbonne ten years earlier and talked to until dawn. She was sure it was him! The date that never happened because she had been late. Because she had hesitated and then gone out after all, running all the way down Boulevard Saint-Michel until she was out of breath, but he hadn't been there. She had waited, alone, out of breath, disheartened, mortified. And he hadn't called her again. Or perhaps he had, later, after she had moved and changed her phone number.

Seeing him again sent a shiver down her spine and made her head spin before her defense mechanism kicked in: she had to hide in case he recognized her, or worse still, in case he didn't recognize her. She desperately wanted to talk to him, but the thought of even catching his eye again confused her, made her doubt herself. She didn't know what to think. She felt worthless, thought she was asocial, uninteresting, ugly.

She half-smiled as he walked toward her. A mutual friend appeared from nowhere, introduced them, and disappeared just as quickly, like magic, because intermediaries or messengers often have to disappear for encounters to happen. It's like they're only directors in a film that is shot and watched once they have created it. And when he smiled at her, she had the feeling he recognized her too.

Vincent had become a man: well-built, muscular, broad shoulders, and confident in his virility. She felt that charm again as he looked at her, or rather, examined her. He still had that distinctive smile, a mysterious sort of expression, somewhere between slightly distant and extreme high regard. Something unsettled her and stripped her of all her resources, like she was a teenager again.

He had a certain beauty, goodness, naturalness, and kindness. Stronger and more mature, even more so than in her memory—he was incredibly attractive. His smile was disarming, and he wasn't fully aware of his charm but was charming nonetheless, with a lock of brown hair over his eyes and the faint scar on his cheek.

They talked for a while about this and that, about him,

about what they were doing and what they expected from life. He mentioned his trips to Brazil, South Africa, Vietnam, Japan, and Australia even, his need to get away, tour the world, and find meaning again after his brother had died, far away from his parents in the hospital where Vincent had spent every evening, with nursing auxiliaries for company. When he had finally returned, under pressure from his family, he had left the socialist party, given up political activism, and abandoned music in favor of finance and consulting. He now worked for a big consultancy group. He missed music and only occasionally played piano in the evening, composed, and sang when he had time. He had become serious a little too soon, a little too fast, but that's how it was, and Amélie realized that he was a man of duty. And what about her? What was her life like? She taught French, didn't travel much. Apart from going to see her parents in Bernay, she had only been as far as Italy, Greece, and London with friends. She worked in a bookstore in Montparnasse and loved being surrounded by books. They talked about that fateful date they had missed ten years earlier. He told her he had been there—but what had happened to her? She had stood him up, right? He had waited for an hour. An hour? She explained she had been late, held back. But held back by what? Well, herself, since deep down you can only be held back by yourself.

And then midnight chimed, interrupting the explanations. A solemn moment, the dawn of the next year, century, and millennium. Everything else was forgotten, and there were kisses all around. They gave each other a peck on the cheek too. She could smell his aftershave, and he sensed a familiar smell that unsettled him. Then there were other people, more kisses and yet more kisses, more best wishes for the new year, more cigarettes, more drugs, more drinks, more dancing. It was the end of a world—perhaps even the end of the world.

As she was leaving around 3 o'clock in the morning, she looked for him, stumbling a little, afraid he had left before she could say goodbye, before she could give him her number, before looking at him one last time. But there he was, sitting on a sofa beside a woman, surrounded by a cloud of smoke. She walked toward him, and he gave her one of his intense looks, like he couldn't take his eyes off her. But what did that look mean? That he wanted to kiss her? Was there passion? Genuine, feigned, or suppressed? Or was it simply a sign to leave, the end of that moment suspended in time? How could she decode so many contradictory messages so quickly? Kiss him perhaps? Accidentally brush his lips as a joke?

She hoped he would see her out. That they would extend the evening, have one last drink, laugh, spend the night together, say they loved each other, get married, have children, have more children, and so on. But he didn't say a word. *Protection* by Massive Attack played in the background as she told him she was leaving, her lips brushing against his ear and her heart pounding.

"You're leaving already?" he mumbled.

"Yes, it's late and my friend Clara has a car. She's dropping me off."

And when he didn't say anything, not a single word, she gave him her number which she had scribbled on a paper napkin.

"Don't lose it," she whispered. And all of a sudden, she kicked herself for having taken the lead, having insisted, having hoped, having made the first move, already regretting the thought of waiting for days for him to call. And then—out of politeness, out of awkwardness, because he wanted to, because he felt the same— he whispered his in number her ear, and she wrote it on her hand.

Half of all the mistakes we make in life are because we act in haste; the other half are because we fail to act at all. That evening, Vincent had done both. He hadn't asked Amélie if they could meet again—or told her he was married. The woman beside him was his wife.

5.

Through a haze of inebriation, Vincent watched Amélie leave. He would have liked to have stopped her. He remembered talking to her and how ten years earlier he had waited for her. So much had changed since then. He had dreamed of becoming a musician, a pianist, but one of his parents' friends had dissuaded him, telling him he wasn't talented enough to become a professional musician. He had also failed the entrance exam for concert pianists, despite spending an entire year preparing with the teacher he'd had all through the conservatory. All those nights arched over the piano, wearing headphones so he wouldn't disturb his family or the neighbors. All those days at the conservatory. And then the day of the entrance exam, when he had seen the others who were so good, so technically accomplished and didn't leave anything to chance, and the few who had the gift of genius. Rising up to the challenge had called for a certain sense of madness, nonchalance, overconfidence even. And perhaps realizing that he didn't actually meet the standard required or have the talent. So he had faced the jury, thinking, *Judge me, crucify me, challenge me. In the next few minutes, make me either the happiest or unhappiest man alive.* Had he really played to the fullest of his ability that day, the way deep down he knew he could? That disappointment, that blighted hope, had shaken his confidence and dreams. He had considered himself a musician, but he wasn't one. He played piano—that was all. His father was right; it was indeed time for him to find another profession. He was the only one left now that his brother had passed away. It had affected him for several months. It had been like giving up who he was, like emptying himself of his very essence. The dream that had grown in his innermost being now had to be covered with a shroud, a shroud of grief over this shattered dream, wounded unrequited love. He loved music, but music did not love him. For several years, he couldn't bring himself to touch a piano or go to a concert. He became despondent. It was too painful. The musician within him had had to give up the belief that emotions were at the heart of life, its very essence.

So he had turned to economics and finance, graduated with a good degree, and got a job with a big American firm—first in Luxembourg, then Paris. His boss said he was doing well and had excellent reviews, even though he didn't have enough of a "corporate" spirit, but he could improve on that. *We don't ask you to think, we ask you to act.* A meeting with HR had been arranged to encourage him to choose a specialization. But the financial crisis had hit and there wouldn't be any promotions; he'd have to wait another year.

He had left the meeting feeling relieved. He was planning to move to the other side of the world and leave it all behind—his father's rants, his mother's laments, his boss's opinions—but then he had met Sophie through mutual friends, over dinner. She was beautiful and taller than him; she talked much more than him, which he liked, being an introvert at heart. She was an actress, which he found enchanting. She was charming and funny, and she helped him rediscover that sense of spirit and imagination he had lost. He invited her out to lunch at a place that had since closed—gone bankrupt or perhaps disappeared by magic—a small, modest restaurant in Rue Saint-André-des-Arts in the heart of Paris Saint-Germain. Their clothes had been like costumes. She had worn a long, low-cut crimson dress. His black pants and white shirt had been on point. They had talked a lot, about this and that, about their plans. About their families, their childhoods. About music, about lyrics. About what makes up the poetry of life. About youth, traveling, São Paulo, Kruger Park, the Mekong River. About politics and the economy, about anything and everything. He didn't have any firm opinions; she did. Family was important to him, along with a certain sense of friendship and loyalty; for her it wasn't. It was clear he liked to help his family, that nothing was too good for them. That he was the kind of guy who liked helping others. That he even tended to put others' needs above his own. Calm, rational, and well-organized in general, he was wary of passion. He was more for unfailing love than crazy love. Or perhaps he simply found it difficult to express his feelings, like he was afraid of suffering. He was impulsive yet knew how to wait, sensitive yet wanted to intellectualize, a little naive, a little cautious, and extremely considerate. She told him about her career as an actor. She'd had a promising start in theater, sang, danced, and had joined a troupe that performed in Paris and elsewhere in France.

Then she took him back to her place, or her parents' place to be precise—a dark, narrow apartment on Rue du Commerce where they had their shop and a piano. He hadn't gone anywhere near one for a long time, like he was afraid of getting burned. He wanted her to like him, so he began to play, and she got caught up in it too. She watched his hands travel over the keys and wished they would touch her face too. He wondered what her gaze meant. Did she want to talk? Had she listened to him play for long enough? Or did she have an appointment? Did it mean she liked him and he should reach out and take her hand, her mouth, her body, her life? She was so beautiful—with her blue eyes, long blond hair, and slim, elegant figure—that he had wanted to take hold of her. And the music unfolding around them, encircling them with grace in the soft light, brought them together. Their thoughts merged in the air in a rare harmony, like they were made for each other. He made peace with himself and loved himself by loving her. He fell in love with her, with the idea of falling in love, and with his father-in-law too. He was a respectable man with a gutsy past, a self-made man who had started from nothing, just a small haberdashery in Rue du Commerce, then a second one, and one thing led to another. He bought more shops, went into stationery, expanded, and made money. Vincent had admired him so much he had wanted to become his son-in-law, to become a little like his son. He had been looking for a father because his own father had been so strict, for a man who could guide him through life and believe in him.

And that's what happened: they went from dates to lunches, lunches to dinners, dinners to parties, parties to nights, nights to years, years of life together. Fate is shaped, it would seem, by one sudden impulse, one tiny thing that makes you take one path or another. A throw of the dice that does not eliminate chance, but rather determines everything.

A few years later, their families met on the square outside Montmartre town hall at the top of the small hill in the winter sun toward the end of the month, the end of the year, the end of the century, the end of the millennium, and the end of his life as a bachelor. She looked like an angel with her lace dress, crown of flowers, blond hair, blue eyes, and red lips. His love for her was one of dedication, devotion, duty, worship—a promise. On the evening of their wedding, an orchestra played a song for her, one he had written and composed himself. Lyrics that recalled the moment he had fallen in love with her, and he had indeed fallen. Yet he was far from imagining just how far. He remembered the moment he had proposed on the balcony of his future father-in-law's apartment, suddenly stirred to do so at the end of a boozy summer evening. How Charles, his best friend and now his best man, ever perceptive, had gravely replied, "I think so too," when Vincent had whispered in his ear: "I think I'm in the process of making a huge mistake."

6.

After the Y2K party, Amélie consulted a clairvoyant to ask if she would ever meet the soulmate she had so desperately been seeking, over hill and dale, across seas and oceans, across every continent. She had spent a year in New York as a French tutor in a student residence. She had crisscrossed Europe with friends, from London to Athens, from Rome to Oslo. She had traveled as far as India, and then to Africa, forever hoping to meet the love of her life, then a man with whom she could have a child, then someone she could love, then a partner with whom she could spend some time, then a one-night stand, and then, in total desperation, a man, any man, for anything, simply the first one she came across. The clairvoyant had told her she was an idealist, attached to friendship and marriage, as well as intellectual pursuits, but she was also a dreamer at heart and generous to the point of exhaustion, which meant she could face a lot of disappointment and disillusionment. Reserved, she found it hard to express her emotions, to confess her love. For that reason,

Amélie would undoubtedly meet her soulmate in her circle of friends.

But there weren't any friends left. Gradually, everyone around her had gotten married, including her exes who had become fathers, and it had become more and more difficult to meet people. She taught a few days a week and spent the rest of her time at the bookstore in Boulevard du Montparnasse. The owner had decided to sell it, and she had put in an offer. She had taken out a loan she would repay with what she earned as a teacher and private tutor. It had an attractive shopfront and a selection of books that was sophisticated, humanist, and intellectual, and it stayed open until 10 o'clock at night. She liked welcoming the customers, some of whom became regulars, then friends with whom she would chat.

From time to time, Amélie heard about Vincent: at dinners or parties, through acquaintances or mutual friends, and in conversations. Each time, her heart skipped a beat so clearly she was afraid others would notice. It was as though the world around her fell silent, and then, in the middle of a great void she would hear: *He works at Deloitte? He's still with his wife? Oh yes, they're closer than ever. They just left for the USA. He's been promoted and is in New York now.* Then, for a while, she would forget him. Especially when she was with someone.

September 11th had made her head spin. She had realized the extent of the shift that had happened, a brutal transition from one era to the next. And out of the blue, she had remembered him. *He was in New York.* Where might he be? Did he work in the Twin Towers? She watched the images on loop again: the planes, the burning towers, the smoke, the disaster. She was petrified.

Time passed and she forgot it all: September 11th, the Twin Towers, the lives destroyed, and even Vincent. She was at a concert one night with a young man when the band began to play "Come As You Are" by Nirvana. For some strange reason, it felt like they were singing for her. *And I swear that I don't have a gun.* Tears welled up in her eyes, so he put his arms around her. He was named Max—he had a restaurant, smiling eyes, stubble, and wore a leather jacket. Afterward, they walked across Paris together, through the Latin Quarter and along the river to the illuminated bridges at Notre-Dame.

On the banks of the Seine, Max and Amélie talked about September 11th, about life, about death. It doesn't matter what you think: the most important thing is time. Time that stopped for them that day. Time that did them the honor of forgetting them, bowing down before this encounter between two hearts that intertwined as they met in that moment.

And as others woke, Max and Amélie were in an apartment overlooking the Seine, growing closer. Smoking, face to face, in an artificial paradise. Tending the other's discontentment with life, fear of the future, anxiety. Smoking weed until they lost themselves, until they forgot who they were, until they laughed and cried about it all. To simply escape and no longer be themselves for an instant, they flew to Venice, and then Verona to watch *Aïda* in the Arena and feel a deep sense of despair.

Amélie let herself have fun and even allowed herself to believe in love for at least a year. They celebrated with a toast in the twilight on the banks of the Seine. She didn't think about happiness in the dark of night, under the stars. She told herself it wasn't important.

On a beach in Sardinia, however, a sense of sadness overwhelmed her one day, like a wave sweeping her soul. She wanted to turn it into something complicated, something infinite, without realizing it was actually the reflection of her own desire, her own soul. As the clairvoyant had said, she was a romantic. She dreamed of marriage, a union, and she was attached to friendship. Her candor and idealism naturally guided her toward humanism. She was a dreamer who got caught up in her own fantasies, so generous that she wore herself out. She found it hard to express her feelings; her strict upbringing had left her reserved by nature. She endured trials with courage and determination and picked herself up again after this little spell of the blues.

A while later, when she heard *"Je ne t'aime plus, mon amour"* by Manu Chao on the radio, she thought of Vincent again. She had heard through mutual friends that he was alive and well—very much alive and well and back in France, in fact. She mentioned it to Clara who got his phone number from an actor with whom she'd had an on-off relationship since that fateful New Year's Eve party.

It was still the same number, the one Amélie had written on her hand and her heart. Under a false pretext, after hesitating for a long time, putting it off, trembling, giving up, giving in, weighing up the pros and cons, preparing a line, then another, and then yet another, asking Clara if it was a good idea, then asking another girlfriend who said the opposite, weighing up the pros and cons again, failing to find the courage, drinking a stiff drink, then a coffee, then another one, shaking again, telling herself it wasn't the right time of day, or the right time in general, putting it off to the next day, then the day after that, forgetting to hope and hoping to forget, she finally called him.

He answered in his warm, deep timbre, and she said it was her, Amélie, Did he remember her? She said she had been thinking about him and asked if he was well, if he still played piano, if he still liked Rilke, and if he was living in Paris. And they arranged to meet for lunch on the Champs Elysée, near his office. Before the date, she went to the hairdresser, did her makeup, got dressed, then changed, again and again, before finally deciding on a summer dress and heels. She felt a sense of confusion, a strange feeling, a sort of tension that was so noticeable it felt like the blood had drained out of her. She was empty, exhausted, yet also ecstatic at the thought of seeing him again.

He arrived at the restaurant wearing a suit and tie— elegant and "corporate." He jumped up and kissed her on the cheek. She wondered if he was attracted to her as much as she was to him. He sat down, smiled, ran his hand through his hair, rearranged the plate, knife, and fork, cracked a few jokes, and ordered everything in one go—starter, main course, and dessert—like a whirlwind, happy. He had a lot to say and talked about his new job, his travels, New York, September 11th when he had been close to the towers, how he had actually escaped by an inch, what the city had been like after the disaster, drained of its lifeblood, its heart and soul. He made her head spin, asked how she was, what she did, and looked into her eyes. Perhaps he was wondering what she wanted from him and why she had suggested this lunch.

What she wanted was him. But admitting that was impossible for a young woman like her who had been brought up well. Their hands brushed against each other accidentally as they reached for a bread roll. They apologized, "No, you take it." A look that made her blush, then silence. The mere sensation of one of his fingers touching her was overwhelming. So she tried asking him a question, "And otherwise, how's life, all fine?" There was a slight moment of awkwardness. Then a moment of grace. A look that lingered, an answer that wasn't one, a confession that couldn't be made. They continued their conversation, about this and that, the economy, politics, morals, elections, the far right which continued to grow, the tension in the neighborhoods on the edges of the city, September 11th again, the event that had turned the world on its head in that bloody explosion, how they didn't really know to what extent yet, the Internet bubble, and finance. "It's all cyclical," he said. "When things go wrong you have to be patient and wait for the next phase." He planned to test the waters as an entrepreneur, to create a startup.

She asked him about the person he was becoming, what was happening in his life, if he was happy. And then he talked about his wife. She was an actor and currently performing in a play, *The Game of Love and Chance.* He asked if Amélie would like tickets. His admiration for his wife seemed infinite. She told herself love was blind—it made you gamble and take risks. But did he have to love her so blindly?

Then, to answer her question, he said he was the happiest man alive. She had understood that, yes. No, she hadn't. He had just become a father. She tried to smile, congratulated him, managed to say it was wonderful news in a tone that wasn't too off key. She didn't think a single treacherous thought, realized it should have been obvious, and told herself she was the tragedienne in this comedy of life that was anything but a romantic comedy. She said nothing, coughed, and almost choked on a bone from the fish that wouldn't go down but rather stayed stuck in her throat, suffocating her until she began to go blue in the face. This time, there was nothing left to say. It was like he had taken her heart and crushed it into a thousand tiny pieces.

7.

The child was called Jules, and Vincent only had eyes for him. Now, all that mattered was whether or not his son had eaten. The day Jules was born, he became Vincent's entire world. Any real intimacy with his wife—who always seemed to be nagging him—had more or less vanished. He worked late and came home exhausted in the evening. He didn't feel like spending time with her anymore and wasn't interested in anything she said either. It was as though all his love had been transferred to his child: his expressions, smiles, hands, and feet. He put him to bed, cradled him for hours, and sang to him. He took him out at the weekend: to the park, to the swimming pool, and for walks in the forest. He would have done anything for Jules. He was the sole breadwinner now because his wife had stopped working. She didn't have much maternal instinct, so he had become both father and mother to the child. He made up for what was lacking and gave his son the affection he needed. Before, he would never have thought that some people turn out to be parents while others don't. That it wasn't natural, innate, or easy. That some people saw children as trophies, or objects you traded, while others watched them grow, amazed at each step, word, expression, or game they played. For him, watching his child was the most wonderful thing in the world. Nothing else really mattered. Neither did his parents, whom he fled. Nor his friends, with whom he no longer shared the same interests. His very existence became the reflection of the beauty he saw in his child.

Jules gave his life meaning. He gave him the energy to fight and work. Vincent was earning good money as a consultant in a different company and had specialized in developing a sector of the future, one he believed in: new technologies. It had been a good idea. He had been rewarded, and his salary had increased. The family moved to the 6th arrondissement, to Rue du Bac in Saint-Germain, not far from Rue de Babylone. There was a small park with French gardens where he liked to take Jules for walks and sit on the lawn beside the vegetable garden—a small green paradise, hidden in the heart of the city, of life, his life.

His wife didn't take care of their apartment either. She didn't like cooking or cleaning. It was as though their roles had been reversed. He was the one who cooked and did the dishes; she could have sat there with a newspaper, smoking a cigar. But it would never have occurred to him to complain. Even though he realized his feelings were no longer as strong as they once were, he respected her. During the fights—which became more frequent—he remained calm and made sure he stayed silent so as not to aggravate matters, which did in fact aggravate matters. He would look to the heavens without saying a word. The only thing he thought about was working even harder for his son. He wanted to treat him, take care of him, and make him as happy as possible. One day, as he was talking to his father-in-law about his shops—the haberdashery and stationery stores were in the red—he came up with the idea that would make them rich: they would use the Internet and the digital revolution to start selling their wares online.

When he met Amélie for lunch that day, he was struck by her beauty. He studied her mouth, her eyes, and her delicate, manicured hands. He watched her fingers dance and her lips move as she talked. When she smiled, he noticed her perfect teeth, disciplined like her. He observed her slightly stiff posture and shoulders that were a little arched, like she was protecting herself. He took in her enthusiasm, laughter, and imagination, and he realized that his heart beat a little faster when he saw her. Something indefinable was happening between them, something that had nothing to do with what they were talking about. A secret language emerged from their bodies and souls. Or from the depths of their hearts no doubt. A sub-text to their apparently ordinary conversation about what they were doing, books, music, France, politics, his travels. But who was she to him? She wasn't his friend, his mistress, or his wife. She was something different, and he wasn't indifferent to her. She was a constant amidst the variables in his existence. Who was she really? He wouldn't have been able to put his finger on it. He wouldn't have allowed himself to put what he felt into words. He was simply living it, excited by it, and yet unaware of it. He didn't analyze this self-evident fact, didn't draw anything from this conversation that was drawn out, or perhaps didn't die out, yet was dying out because it wasn't saying, *Can't you see I'm dying to love you?*

8.

Thirty-five years old—it's worth celebrating, even if you're still single. On May 9, 2003, Amélie was celebrating her birthday with Clara and a group of friends in Rue de la Roquette in the Bastille neighborhood. She had brought her camera and asked the man at the next table to take a photo of the group. The smiling young man—straight-backed, distinguished looking, light-colored eyes behind his round glasses, and a pleasant face despite his premature baldness—obliged. But the camera didn't work. Unruffled, considerate, and charming, he suggested taking a photo with his cellphone, a Nokia with a built-in camera. Amélie agreed, and he asked for her number so he could send the photo, promising to delete both the photo and phone number immediately, to which Amélie replied, "Oh, that's a pity, you should keep them." So he texted her, she replied, and they chatted for a few days, friendly flirting in those early days of text messaging. He invited her out for dinner at the restaurant near the Bastille where they had first met. They met up a few more times, and one evening he kissed her on the Pont des Arts. He took her to Cabourg for the weekend, and then one day his apartment caught fire. He didn't have a single piece of clothing or furniture left, so it was only natural that he moved his last few remaining possessions into her place, and they began to live together.

Fabrice had almost finished his surgical residency with a team that worked hard and then partied hard in the on-call rooms at night. One day, he invited Amélie to observe an open-heart surgery. She watched him open and cut into a thorax. She saw how he held the heart in his hands, the heart he had stopped in order to operate on it, how he changed a blocked artery by replacing it with a vein taken from the leg. Then, after grating the veins to the heart, he returned it to its functioning state. It was the most impressive thing she had ever seen. She was both excited and overwhelmed at having seen life face death with her own eyes. She felt like she had witnessed an absolute form. It was as though she had seen her own heart beating again for this man she admired, this man she loved with all her heart, a heart that had been revived in his hands. But what about him? When she had almost fainted, he had told her that to be able to operate, you had to cut yourself off from your feelings. "And everything else?" she had asked. As for everything else: he said he had never fallen in love.

He won her over with his intelligence, his ability to listen, and his powers of seduction. He was calm; she was anxious. He was practical; she was a dreamer. He was reassuring and strong. Up close, he wasn't particularly handsome with his slightly tight-lipped mouth and large forehead, but he had green eyes and a beautiful smile. He was rather attractive and most definitely a ladies' man. And that's how she fell for him after wandering from man to man with the strange impression they were all interchangeable, all similar, and all had the same effect on her. At least she wasn't bored with him. He left early in the morning and came home late in the evening. His days were intense—he saved lives and held hearts in his hands, including hers. This is why when she asked him to propose—and he then proposed—she said yes.

Outside the town hall in the 6th arrondissement, their parents, relatives, and friends gathered in Place des Grands-Hommes dominated by the Pantheon and its noble characters. Brothers, sisters, and cousins. They had planned a drinks reception at the hotel on the square. It rained as the guests arrived. Like all those weddings of her friends she had attended for years, she could have been the witness, the maid of honor, a sister twice, a friend, a cousin, single, or an ex. She had helped with the preparations, been at the bachelorette parties and ceremonies, wore a dress, brought cakes to celebrations, and been there for the first children. Her family had traveled from Normandy. Her parents dressed in their Sunday best, as well as her sisters and friends. Clara was her witness in a violet hat and a scandalously tight mauve dress, cradling her new dog in her arms as it rained cats and dogs.

The sun shone through the raindrops, the sidewalk glistened brightly, and her heart raced. She was bursting with joy.
She thought marriage was an accomplishment in her life
as a woman, the most precious thing she could desire.
After the drizzle stopped, a rainbow appeared on the horizon—a symbol of the new life she was creating for herself.
A life together in that small attic apartment they shared in
the Marais. A short distance away, the dark Seine glistened as the sun set on its sparkling waters, with a giant
Eiffel Tower cloaked in darkness plunging into in it, the
moving water caressing its shadow. Paris had been rava-
ged by a summer of heatwaves, the architects Libeskind
and Childs had been selected to redesign the World Tra-
de Center Twin Towers in New York, a packed bus had
crashed in Columbia, and the planet Mars had never been
closer to Earth—this Earth that had continued to turn
after closing the chapter on the previous millennium.
And closed, too, were the eyes of the newlyweds in the
twilight at the end of that rainy wedding day, a day that
had been joyous, forgetful, fabulous, and disastrous.

9.

On July 6, 2005, it was raining as they drove back to Paris. Jules was asleep in the backseat of the car when Sophie began to shout. She told Vincent she didn't feel safe, that he was a bad driver and was going too fast, too slow, too everything. It was always too much of everything with her. Without warning, he stopped at a highway rest area, got out of the car, and slammed the door, like he couldn't take it anymore.

"What's gotten into you? Do you feel sick?" she asked, joining him.

Jules had woken up and was quietly watching his parents through the car window.

"I can't take it anymore, Sophie. I'm suffocating. I feel like I'm dying," said Vincent.

"It must be the oysters. You know very well you're allergic."

"No, it's not the oysters. It's . . . you," he said.

"Me? What do you mean?" Sophie asked. They stood there in the rain, in the parking lot, beside the car.

"I can't take these fights anymore. I can't take your shouting anymore."

"But what's gotten into you? Is this a panic attack? Did you take your antidepressants this morning?" she quizzed him.

"Yes, and that's it—I took them. I can't go on like this. I've lost all meaning."

"Meaning of what?"

"I've lost all meaning in my life. I'm confused. I don't know. I don't know who I am anymore," he replied.

"It must be a mid-life crisis," she said. "But you're only thirty-seven, it's a bit early."

"I don't care about getting older. Actually, I do want to be old. I want it all to be over."

"You need to increase your dose. Make an appointment with Dr. Bansard."

"It's not the antidepressants. I don't feel good with you anymore. That's all," said Vincent.

"Really? You don't feel good with me anymore? So what were you expecting?" she asked.

"We're not a couple anymore, Sophie. We're you and me, but we're not a couple."

"Well then, what's a couple, for you?" she asked.

"A couple is two people who love each other. Not two people who put up with each other," he explained.

"The one putting up with the other one is me. Can't you see how much your depression is affecting me? It's hard carrying someone else."

"I don't think . . ."

"What?" she asked.

"I don't think I'm depressed," Vincent said.

"Oh really? And what does your psychologist say?"

"He doesn't say anything. He listens to me. I'm not depressed, Sophie. I just can't stand your shouting anymore—your screaming, your bad moods, the way you treat me. We don't love each other anymore. I don't love you anymore," he answered.

"You've got someone else, haven't you?" Sophie asked.

"That's funny," he replied. "You've shared my life for more than ten years and you still haven't understood who I am."

"And you're going to tell me, are you?"

"I'm an idealist," said Vincent.

"Oh yes, an idealist! That's why you're running away," shouted Sophie.

"Running away from what?" Vincent asked.

"From me, from us. From everything. Above all, from yourself," she added.

"That's true. I think we've reached the end," he said.

"The end of what?" Sophie asked.

"The end of a cycle."

"But what's gotten into you? Do you think you're giving a PowerPoint presentation?" she asked him.

"I'm sorry, I just can't find the words. But I think you get the idea," he answered.

"The idea? What? That you want to leave? That you've met someone?"

"No, there isn't anyone," Vincent repeated again.

"Listen here, Vincent. I'm not going to let you destroy our family. I'm on my own with Jules most of the time. You don't do anything; I do everything at home! So you're going to take responsibility and get on with the job of being a husband and father. Even if it doesn't make you happy. Like me. Like everyone else."

"Work, yes, make cash and get the job done. That's what I'm doing, for you, for both of you. But all of a sudden, it feels like none of that makes sense. I'm suffocating, don't you understand?"

He had felt like crying when he'd heard *"Je ne t'aime plus, mon amour"* come up on Pop Idol the night before as he had watched TV with Jules. He no longer loved his love. But he did love his son, more than anything in the world. Why? How had he come to this point?

And had he ever really loved her? Or had he just gotten caught up in the relationship due to pressure, cowardice, and social obligations—because there had been the expectation he would get married? It had been too perfect: she was beautiful, attractive, intelligent, all over him, and wanted to marry him. He couldn't refuse such a gift, even though deep down it had troubled him and he had tried to get himself out of it, but to no avail, failing to due to his lack of courage and his sense of duty.

"You've got a mistress. It's obvious. Go on, admit it," she shouted.

"No. You should know I don't. I'm not that kind of man."

"What kind?" she asked.

"The kind to have a mistress."

"Oh yes, of course. You're not like the others. You don't get caught up in the tribulations of life. You're capable of moving mountains for your family. That's what you're saying, right?"

"I've never had an affair. You have, yes. But I haven't."

"What're you saying?" Sophie asked.

"I know that you cheat on me," he replied.

"What makes you say that?"

"I've been told. You've been seen at the theater. You don't even try to hide it," he said.

So yes. She'd had lovers, of course. And that had cost her, too.

She'd had to change her opinion: about herself, about the life she had pictured for herself. Accept she would never be the actor she had thought she was, but rather become the actor in her own life. Force herself to lie. Lie better, lie more often. Deception as a game, a vice. Lie out of pity, out of envy, out of hate, lie because she detested herself and the other, and for love too, because she didn't want to hurt him. That was the reason she hadn't left, because she still loved him.

He had come home early one evening, and she had even introduced her lover to him, like a friend. He hadn't even noticed. It was as though he couldn't feel anything, never expressed a single emotion. He wasn't a moron, but his sentimental blind spot made him blind, or naive perhaps. He was like a second child, a difficult teenager she had raised along with his little brother.

"You don't love me anymore. That's why I cheat on you," she said. "You don't look at me anymore. You don't listen to me. You don't hear me."

The next day, Vincent packed a suitcase with a few of his personal belongings and left for London to run the company he had set up with his father-in-law. His success allowed him to escape, to travel, and whenever he came back it was for his son. He wasn't like his colleagues; he didn't take the opportunity to go on dates or cheat on his wife. He didn't like that sort of coarse behavior. He didn't go out with them or join in their conversations. He was devoted.

The landscape whizzed by as he chatted with the passenger in the next seat. The guy told him about Meetic, an online dating agency that matched men and women using extremely detailed criteria. His travel companion had signed up and spent a lot of time meeting women online, then in real life. For the rest of the journey, he replayed the film of his own marriage in his mind and thought about how he had never considered cheating on his wife, yet somehow felt a sense of regret at never having done so.

He checked his phone. There was a message from Sophie: *I love you Vincent, I'm thinking about you, about us. About our family.* What did that *I love you* mean? Was it a reminder, a request, a promise? Or perhaps it meant I still love you, our relationship isn't over, let's try again? Or perhaps it was a cry for help that was more of a command, love me, love me again? Was it a sign of an implicit commitment, a word, responsibility for a family that he couldn't, that he shouldn't break up? Not least for his son's sake. Love, stronger than passion. Children, stronger than love. And oneself, the least strong of all.

His wife and her gentle, magnificent, dazzling smile. His wife as an extension of himself, like part of him, like his child. His wife who was his day-to-day, his bed, his evening meals and his breakfasts, his Sunday morning excursions, his memories—his past.

His wife to whom he spoke on the phone; her voice resonating and reasoning with words that sounded familiar, that imprisoned him in his house, their home, his home, because the husband of this woman, well, that was him. His wife who waited for him, ready to go into battle. His wife who screamed at him and at their son, who reminded him of his duty, his memory, his cupboard, his couch, his wife, his mother, a woman too, from long ago, like his wife who he married long ago and made his own, outstanding in his detachment. His princess wife of various cleaners, homebody and assistant, women of yesterday, mothers and grandmothers, and his wife in his bed, his wife who gave him a child, his wife who shouted on the telephone, this woman who was no longer his wife.

And him: an upstanding man who had built his life around his family. A man who had married because he had fallen in love. And who, out of love, stayed. A man who had given everything he had: his time, his life, his house, his money, a child, a company. Everything it had been in his power to give, he had offered her, but that hadn't made her happy because the only thing he couldn't give her was his heart.

He got up early the next day and wandered aimlessly around London. It was raining, so he went into a café where he watched a couple gazing into each other's eyes. A couple who looked like they were in love, a French couple. The French were the only ones who put love above everything else, he thought. Out of the blue, he remembered that girl, Amélie. He wondered why she had sent him a text message after so long. Then he wondered what she was doing, what her life was like, and why he had remembered her at this stage in his life. He felt like calling her, so he got out his phone. Just as he was about to dial her number, he heard a blast. Explosions in the King's Cross underground station, right next to the cafe where he was sitting, not long before he had been due to catch the Tube to his meeting. Everything around him began to spin. In only a few minutes he would have been there, too. He smelled smoke, gagged, and blacked out.

10.

It was love at first sight on July 2, 2006.

When Amélie saw him, she thought he was gorgeous, perfect—despite the fact he didn't have much hair, was a bit wrinkly, looked exhausted, and wouldn't exactly have ranked as one of the cutest guys around. He was calm, content, relaxed. She thought he looked wise, that he had something to teach her; she didn't know how true that would be. He would teach her who he was, who she was— and then who they were together.

That day, they spent the night together. Their bodies met before their minds did. They were one; it was clear. She loved the sensation of their sweat mingling. It was so hot it was impossible to cool off. His mouth, his hands taking hold of her, his body nestled against hers. He look-ed at her without blinking, staring, short-sighted, a little blind, bewitched by her smell. That's when she realized it was the start of an incredible love story.

That summer was like a sweet, sweaty mirage. She didn't see anyone else. Everyone was exhausted by the heat, holed up at home; only a lucky few had left the city to cool down elsewhere. But not them. From time to time, she got up, drank some water, ate something, and returned to him. The surreal heat added a certain fieriness to their relationship. It was like a bubble, an airlock, a cocoon, their own personal parallel universe.

He spoke to her through his eyes, his gestures. She was the more talkative one for once, the one who spoke words, words of love. He inhaled her, sought her, couldn't cope without her or contact with her body. They were inseparable, permanently joined by an invisible thread. His need for her was so great that he often woke her during the night. When they got up in the morning, the day had already started. She contemplated him and couldn't get over seeing him there, beside her; it was simply wonderful.

His love for her was so strong and his need for her so urgent that she never worried he wouldn't like her. In his eyes, she was the most beautiful woman in the world, despite her messy hair and lack of makeup. He didn't care what she wore either. He loved her for being her. He didn't know who she was or what her life was like; little by little, he discovered it all. He accepted everything about her—apart from when she left him, even briefly.

Sometimes it was almost too much. She needed to breathe, get away, collect her thoughts, but he wouldn't let her. As soon as she left the room, he would sink into despair. He couldn't stand it. He didn't want her to leave; he wanted her all to himself. He was jealous, impulsive, and tyrannical. She didn't like it when anyone else approached him either, touched him, held him, or embraced him. They belonged to each other. Alone in the world, they didn't need anyone else. What kind of love is as crazy as that kind of love?

Yet September arrived. The city filled up again, people went back to work. The temperature fell while the wind chased away the Indian summer, so she decided to leave him. Initially, he protested. He shouted, screamed, and ranted. He stayed there, waiting for her all day. All he did was wait for her to return. Then he resigned himself to the fact and found consolation in the arms of another woman.

But when she saw him again in the evening, it was as though the entire universe opened up for them, and with just one kiss they were tenderly united. She softly whispered sweet nothings in his ears and stroked his hands. They stared into each other's eyes, and she lost herself entirely as she gazed at her baby.

She would have done anything for him. He had her backed into a corner and woke her six times a night since the day he had been born. She gave in to his every caprice, every outburst, all of his impetuous demands. He dominated her and demanded the ultimate sacrifice. She did everything for him. Nursed him every five minutes if necessary, fed him, washed him, dressed him, and took him to the pediatrician; watching him smile was her reward. She would have braved any danger in the world for him, bought him the moon. Everything else seemed of secondary importance now. She knew the joy of loving and being loved in return. She was everything to him, and he was everything to her. In no time, he had won her over, body and soul: he had become the center of her life and had her full attention every minute, second, and hour of the day. Every thought she had revolved around him. There was no one else in the world apart from him.

Her pregnancy had been a lonely period. Fabrice had worked a lot and no longer seemed interested in her, looking only at her in a dismissive way, with disgust even. It was strange how he had left her alone, gone off on holiday with his friends, and regarded her with scorn and condescension. His work took up all his time and made him anxious, which explained why he came home late, but not why he preferred to go out with his friends as opposed to her. He was tired but happy to have a home, a wife, a dinner on the table, domestic comfort, and a glass of wine, which became half a bottle, then a bottle, then a glass of whiskey, and so on.

Even when he was home, he was absent. He took no interest in either of them and didn't even go into the nursery to see his son. He shut himself away in his office and didn't come out. He was miserable and sad, didn't have anything to talk about, and proved to be rude and vulgar, scornful. He couldn't even manage to show interest in her for five minutes a day. Anything more than that was too much for him. He didn't take them away on vacation. On Sundays, he closed himself up in his study and chain-smoked. He didn't pay for anything, or did his best to pay for as little as possible. He didn't pay for the hospital, or a single diaper for the baby, never bought the groceries—he only took care of himself. Not one gift, not an iota of attention. He didn't care about a single thing. He thought about one person alone: himself. He was alive, or rather pretended to be alive, but he was like a zombie, so traumatized by life that he had decided to give up on the very idea of existing, simply pulling the wool over his eyes to put on a good front. Amélie realized that was all he had used her for. She felt trapped. She thought their relationship was over, that there wasn't the slightest hope they would stay together, so she asked him for another child.

She didn't want her son to be alone with Fabrice. She loved her son so much that she graciously endured her husband's disdain. She loved her son so much that she decided to do everything she could to make sure he had a little brother or sister who would be with him, a loyal companion for when they would have to shuttle back and forth after the divorce she had begun to consider more and more often. He would have a shoulder to cry on, a friend to talk to. Above all, she couldn't imagine her child being alone with his father, who had started to drink to mask his boredom, or despair. She discovered empty whiskey bottles in the study. Alcohol disinhibited him, and she had found him lying dead drunk in the lounge a few times, with their son watching him through the bars of his play crib, puzzled.

One evening, she asked Fabrice if they could talk, like she was setting up an appointment or medical consultation. She showed him the positive pregnancy test; they looked at each other, filled with dismay. They knew it meant a few more years together even though they didn't want to be, having reached the point where they hated each other. It was to be a difficult pregnancy, not because she was taking care of her son alone or because she was working, but because her husband was becoming more and more unbearable. He hated her: it was as though motherhood had sickened him of her. He projected his own mother onto her, a woman he couldn't stand. He wasn't interested in her bookstore—he never set a foot in it—or her friends or her family: anything to do with her made his hair stand on end. He came home in the evenings, never a smile to be seen, and dumped his backpack with its contents that remained a mystery—was there perhaps a stethoscope?

One day, she called to ask when he'd be home. He said he was still at the hospital, but when she went down to the cafe below their apartment to meet a friend, she saw him. There he was, drinking a beer with a friend, smiling. He was fleeing her and the children, and he had all sorts of excuses: the hospital, consultations, and trips to congresses from which he returned happy, open boxes of Viagra in his bag. He was even more absent when he was there than when he wasn't.

He could have continued like that for another twenty years, his entire life even. He kept up appearances: a family, a wife, a relationship. He didn't see or hear anything and wasn't interested in anything, apart from judging, criticizing, or demeaning others. He only opened his mouth to speak ill of others. He had a death drive according to her psychoanalyst, whom she saw more and more often in order to find a way to tolerate life, to find a way out because she couldn't picture divorcing him, yet was unable to resign herself to staying with him either.

Amélie often wondered how he managed to live like that. Sometimes she felt like she was part of a pack, a group of mammals that are together because they decided to reproduce.

One evening, when he was holed up in his study in a cloud of hash and alcohol, she put the children to bed and went back into the living room. The vintage gumdrop iMac computer was on the small table, like a huge pink candy. She turned it on, and then Fabrice appeared, high as a kite. He was always in a good mood whenever he smoked, his eyes rolled back into his head, pupils dilated, in high spirits, nice almost.

"So you still don't have a Facebook account?"

"A what?" she asked.

"Facebook! Poor thing. You have to keep up," he replied.

"I don't know how. Can you show me?"

"Yeah, sure. At least it'll give you something to do!" he guffawed.

Still holding his joint, he sat down and opened a new

window displaying the blue and white homepage. He registered Amélie's name and e-mail address.

"There you go," he said and headed back to his study. "Have fun, darling."

She looked at the computer screen and the Facebook icon. The account set up with her first name and married name, Amélie Maurel, was already suggesting friends to add, accept, and consider. She wondered whom she could add as a friend. She looked in her contacts, and her heart skipped a beat when she saw Vincent Brunel's name. She searched for him and found him: a profile photo where he was smiling and had short hair and stubble, posts from a conference, an announcement, trips to various countries for work, photos from vacations, his son, him and his wife under palm trees. He had more than 100 friends, which looked like a lot to her. Curious, she sent him a friend request. He replied immediately. Magic! Just like that, you could contact someone else and connect, without the need for a telephone, without saying a single word, without getting in a car or catching the metro or the bus, with absolutely nothing at all; all you needed was the Holy Spirit of Facebook. A ubiquitous form of life on Earth had just been born!

How are you Amélie? he wrote on Facebook Messenger.
I'm fine, and you? she replied.
Great.
Nice to find you on the Web!
What do you do? Are you in Paris? he asked.
Yes, I'm here. And you? she wrote back.

Me too.

And that's how, on December 12, 2008, they arranged to meet up.

11.

On December 16, 2008, Amélie did the math. They hadn't seen each other for five years. The last time they had met, he told her he had just become a father. Looking at her reflection in the bathroom mirror, she noticed the weight she had gained after the pregnancies, a few wrinkles, the gray hairs; she took stock of how time was passing.

She went to the hairdresser, had her hair cut and colored, got out a suit, then a dress, then a skirt and sweater, and then another pair of pants, stepped into heels to make her look slimmer, did her makeup, squirted a puff of perfume like she was going out for the evening, changed again, and then finally slipped into a pair of jeans and a T-shirt and went to meet him at a restaurant near his office in Rue de Ponthieu.

Vincent was there, on time as usual, still the same, dressed in a dark suit and white shirt, no tie. He hadn't changed much, apart from his hair which was starting to go gray around the temples. He still had that smile in his eyes—those eyes that looked right into hers. Cheerful, extremely kind, funny. He asked what had become of her; it had been a long time since they'd last met! So she told him about her children. She had spent the last three years either pregnant or breastfeeding, getting caught up in playtimes, bath times, mealtimes, trips to the park, or shopping, while still running her bookstore. She said that although she was married, she was living like a single mother, taking care of everything, exhausted, so tired she felt faint. During the day, she wondered how other mothers managed to look so good when they dropped their children off at school in the mornings. Perhaps they weren't on their own as much as she was, or perhaps they had help or a husband or partner who was around, loving and normal, yet she wouldn't have wanted to see her own husband more often.

"How old are your children?" he asked.

"Arthur is two-and-a-half, and Pauline is one."

"And what about your parents? Do they still live in Normandy?"

"Yes. But I don't see them much anymore to be honest," she said.

"I don't see mine very often either," he replied. "I distanced myself a bit. After my grandfather passed away, last year."

"I'm sorry to hear that. I remember you were close to him," she said.

"Yes, it was sad, but . . . it's okay now. And your husband, he's a doctor, right?"

She didn't tell him she couldn't stand either Fabrice

or his parents who were full of good intentions, that her marriage was just a sham and nothing but pain, or that motherhood was killing their relationship, which had already been worn down by life together and the abuse she received from the person she had thought she loved for a fraction of an instant, a moment of madness or hormonal panic. She was considering divorce but couldn't quite picture leaving her children every other weekend or, worse still, every other week since that was the current trend in court. She didn't confide in him that her husband was depressed even though he believed he was fine. And better still, not only did he not know it, but he believed he was a king, a half-god, scornful and arrogant, who used people before rejecting them, like he had done with her, not sincere in the least. Selfish, opportunist, fatalist, pathetic.

"My husband," she mumbled. "He's the opposite . . . of you."

He looked at her, taken aback, embarrassed almost at hearing this confession.

"What do you mean?" he asked.

"Marriage is a lottery. A lucky dip. You don't really know what you'll get. I ended up with a dark soul, a bone-dry heart, and wallet too."

"He never gives you gifts?" Vincent asked.

"No, never."

"Flowers?"

"It's been a long time since a man gave me flowers," she said.

"I'd give you white roses."

"Is that a future or a conditional?" she asked.

"What?"

"The tense in your sentence."

"The conditional future, Little Miss Teacher."

"That doesn't exist," she replied.

"No?"

"Why white?"

"White roses are for friendship," he explained.

"Really?"

"What did you think they were for?"

"Sincere feelings," she said.

She looked at him, and he held her gaze for an instant. She was tempted to take his hand, pull him toward her, for everything to change radically, in that very instant, and to finally say what she had never dared say before, that she didn't want anyone but him, that the tempo of her life had been set by the times she had waited for him, and the times she had seen him. That she had never stopped thinking about him, even though sometimes she did stop thinking about him. That he was like a recurring dream, background music, a sigh in her heart, the horizon she never reached, an ideal. That to pass the time, she had gotten married, had two children, and built up a bookstore. But all of that . . . was nothing compared to a minute with him. That it was enough for her, and that beyond those times, she was on the edge. That the present was impossible, that their connection continued through the past and the future—but which future? And what if time didn't exist? A few words barely uttered could be an eternity. And in those moments, nothing else existed. Her heart was in pieces whenever she saw him; the world came back to life. And afterward, she was nothing, like a void. Why did every minute with him take on the color of eternity, resonate disproportionately, and everything else seem pathetic and identical afterward? Would she ever find an answer to all those questions? Why did they hold each other in such high regard?

She moved her hand toward him, but at that crucial moment he reached for his phone and showed her a photo: of a baby. Hideous, toothless, fat, deep-set eyes, drooping cheeks, and absurd little ringlets on the top of its head. A horrible, hateful, thickset, chubby-cheeked little infant that looked like a fat marshmallow; an abominable little rug rat force-fed rice cereal in its bottles, spoon-fed yogurts, and little jars of green and orange food; a hilarious, demonic little Buddha; a terrible, atrocious, repugnant baby! The kind that rips your perineum during labor before piercing your eardrums with their cries; that wake you up every hour during the night like megalomaniac psychopaths, hysterically manic-depressive; that pee just after you have changed their diaper; one of those four-legged stomachs that vomit revolting, half-digested, sickening milk puree over your new dress; whose sole purpose is none other than to destroy your life, your life as a woman, as an adult, your relationship; the kind that grow up and when they're teenagers who have learned to haltingly read a few words, only leave their bedrooms to tell you that you're the worst mother in the world; the kind that no longer recognize you when you're old, apart from shedding crocodile tears on your grave. All in all, they're born crying and bury you crying—those revolting babies!

"My daughter . . ." he said. "I'm crazy about her!"

"I didn't know," she mumbled. "How old is she?"

"Nine months. What a bundle of joy!"

"Yes, what a bundle of joy," she sighed.

He looked at her, overwhelmed. "She's the best thing ever. The best thing in my entire life."

Dreams are too, she felt like saying.

"And love?" she asked.

"That's it—love," he replied, "Pure love."

"What's that?" she asked, shaking.

"You'll see. Now you have children, you'll understand what it really means to love someone else."

When she heard those words, she thought she was going to faint. *And she realized that he had never loved his wife.*

12.

On August 3, 2009, Vincent nodded off as he watched the horizon. In a sad state, he regressed to his childhood, rediscovering feelings buried in his subconscious. His daydream carried him back to a vacation with his parents and older brother in Spain when his mother had them paint stones she had collected on the beach. They had used paintbrushes and marker pens to decorate them with cheerful blue and white images, the colors of the sea.

He lingered in the daydream that was so close to reality, floating between the imaginary and the real. He missed his brother at times. Maybe he could have shared his doubts and worries with him. He could barely talk to his parents; they wouldn't have understood his qualms. Charles was in London, so he didn't see him much either—he felt alone, extremely alone. What does it take to be born anew, to open oneself up to life again? He had one pleasure, however: letting go, giving in, yielding to the delight of doing nothing.

Every morning, he took his antidepressants, and every evening, he took pills to help him sleep, to escape. His daily nap was his inner sanctum, the moment when he abandoned himself, or pulled himself together. The ultimate transgression of the depressed, the guilty, the addicts, the ones searching for distractions while asleep. The dropouts, the antisocial, the losers. Even sleep was supposed to be productive—nothing was to be redundant. He locked the door at work so he could sleep, embarrassed. And if he hadn't been in that particular state of mind created by his pills, if he hadn't had that need, he would never have granted himself this unacceptable vice. It was greater than him. It was more than an irrepressible desire. It was a need deep within him that he couldn't resist. He yearned for it in a way he couldn't control; it swept him up and carried him away—and sometimes he wished he wouldn't return.

***

Lying across the armchair with one hand over her eyes, Amélie allowed herself to groggily succumb to a slumber filled with wild, baroque, kaleidoscopic, psychedelic dreams. As she dozed, that recurring nightmare she'd been having for years came back: she and Fabrice were in a car that went out of control on a bridge, fell into the water, and slowly sank. She woke up panting, feeling like she had returned from some faraway place. She knew the dream was a metaphor for her life. She was in limbo and had to snap out of it, return to reality, look around her, drag her heavy body up, feel her full weight again. It was like she had forgotten everything while she was asleep: the house she had rented for the summer break with her husband, her children, her worries, her despair.

***

Vincent woke up and stood up to look out at the sea from the balcony. They had rented a small house behind the village square. She was the one who had insisted. He never wanted to go away on vacation, so they usually stayed in Paris in August—or she went without him. He'd take her to the station with the children, and then go home, happy to finally be on his own, freed of a weight. He didn't like being with them, and even when he was there, he was absent, shut away in his study. The children returned in September, tanned and happy. They were growing up: Jules was eight and Joséphine was three.

The previous evening, a babysitter had come over, and he and Sophie had gone out for dinner. The restaurant on the small square was decorated in an outdated romantic style. Sophie wore a light summer dress and sandals, and she ordered a glass of rosé. She had regained her slender shape and looked radiant, like when they had first met.

"It's our first dinner out together in a long time," she had remarked. "Do you know many couples who can really go out for dinner like lovers? Our relationship is strong, and we're strong as a couple."

He had been drinking too, something he didn't normally do. They had talked about work, about this and that, and she seemed happy.

Then they had wandered across the square to a bench and sat down. He held her hand, and she rested her head on his shoulder.

***

Amélie looked out at the sea sparkling in the sun. Fabrice had fallen asleep beside her, Arthur was playing in his room, and Pauline was taking a nap. She heard a rattle: text messages arriving on her husband's cellphone lying on the bedside cabinet. The iPhone was within easy reach. She entered the code, her finger trembling. She tried his date of birth and it worked, of course. The cellphone lit up.

She was aware of the significance of the moment. She was about to discover his life and find answers to all her questions. She was about to enter the innermost thoughts and mind of the person who lived at her side, the one who was the closest yet furthest away. But the situation required composure; she needed to slow down her racing heart. First, she had to put it in airplane mode to deactivate the ringtone that might wake him. She got up and went into the bathroom. *No one knows you the way it does*, thought Amélie. No one else knows everything you do. Even if you told your life story, you'd forget entire sections of it, but this thing never forgets. It keeps everything, even things you deleted, stored, archived; it owns you more than you own it.

It's you. In my hands.

Where should she start?

The photos were the easiest. She was immediately drawn to pictures of their children on vacation. Lots of photos of Arthur, only a few of Pauline. Videos that showed what a wonderful father he was. Videos of him getting his son to do his homework, which he had in fact only done once in his entire life. And more of Fabrice, overacting the bond. The best friend dad, incredibly nice, overexcited, and making fun of the "annoying" mother. Then Fabrice with a group of friends in Asia somewhere, partying, showing off, completely out of sync with the other scenes he had filmed. Then pictures of a hotel room in Monaco, videos in night clubs where you couldn't see a thing, presentations at a medical conference where he talked in a pedantic manner befitting of one of Molière's doctors. And then, all of a sudden, she was drawn to a photo of a little girl who strangely resembled Pauline but wasn't. *Another little girl.*

Amélie's heart was pounding furiously, and her hands were trembling. Who was that little girl? Shaking, Amélie read through the text messages as cold sweat ran down her spine and her heart pounded, afraid Fabrice would wake up before she knew the truth.

She started with the text messages exchanged with a woman called Lisa, including one particular thread.

I really get the impression that some women just need to be in touch via text message, are you like that?

No, why?

I only meet crazy women on the Net. Are you a bit crazy too?

No, but I need to be able to vibe with someone.

Same here. It's not easy to vibe with someone, right?

***

When he woke from his nap, Vincent heard something vibrate. It was Sophie's cellphone. She had gone to the pool with the children. He was tempted to get it and take a look. Who was this woman really, his wife? And what kind of life did she lead? Was she still cheating on him? He reached out, lifted the phone, and heard a noise. He had no other option but to hide it under the sheet.

Sophie was back.

"You haven't seen my cellphone, have you?" she asked.

"No, why?"

"Oh no reason," she said, giving him an odd look. "I must have left it somewhere. Unless you took it?"

"I don't have it," he replied, casually. "I really don't."

He felt the cellphone vibrate in his hand.

"So what's that noise?"

***

Amélie took the cellphone into the living room. She heard the ringtone, and a name appeared, *Lisa*. A few minutes later, a message with a photo arrived.

Chloé would like to meet her dad.

A photo of the little two-year-old girl, big green eyes, tight, thin lips, and curly hair; she looked like Fabrice.

All of a sudden, she noticed Fabrice standing at the door. He was awake and watching her. Amélie immediately ran out into the garden. She slipped out of the dress she had pulled on over her swimsuit. Still holding the cellphone, she jumped into the middle of the pool.

"What are you doing?" asked Fabrice. "Are you crazy?"

"Who is this?" she asked, showing him the photo on the cellphone.

"I don't know," he answered. "What are you talking about?"

"If you don't tell me who this is, I'll throw your phone in the water," she threatened.

She waved the phone around and pretended to drop it in the pool.

"Who is the little girl in this photo?" she asked.

"Give me that back right now. I'm telling you, I need it for work. There might be an emergency."

"An emergency? On vacation?" She waved the cellphone over the water. "Who is Lisa?" she asked.

"Lisa is . . . a nursing auxiliary. Okay? She helps me."

"Helps you do what?" Amélie asked. Beside her, Fabrice was getting agitated, mad, and demanding she give him his phone.

"Go on then. Who is Lisa?"

"Well, she's crazy. She jumped me," explained Fabrice.

"When? How?"

"It's because of you," he said. "Have you looked at yourself?" he asked in an arrogant, condescending tone full of scorn. Quaking and in a terrible rage, she had understood.

"The little girl, she's your daughter?" she asked.

"What are you talking about?"

"Looking at her, there's hardly any doubt, is there? That girl is your daughter, isn't she?"

"I don't care about Lisa, or her daughter. I've got nothing to do with them. Get it? She had a child behind my back. She has to take responsibility. You're family. Once you've understood that, we can move on, you and me."

***

A few hours later, Vincent was sitting in a cafe with Sophie's cellphone, looking at her Facebook profile where she chatted with the lovers she met online. Sophie smiling, Sophie in a swimsuit, on the beach, at drunken parties, with her girlfriends, then pregnant. Sophie who had given birth to a little girl. Sophie, Sophie, Sophie.

***

Her life was one huge mess built on quicksand, and she was stuck in it with her young children, without the slightest clue what the future would be like!

Who would have thought her husband had had a child with that young woman, Lisa? That he'd done everything possible to get her to have an abortion, even going as far as offering her 1,000 dollars compensation before abandoning her, along with his own daughter?

***

"I really, really want you to understand. I want to explain, honestly. I need to seduce, to feel like I exist for an instant. Can't you just try to understand? It's nothing against you. And anyway, it's not important. It doesn't mean anything at all. It's just something I do for myself because I need to. If you could just understand, then we can start over together."

***

And all of a sudden, Amélie remembered that in the middle of the pathetic bunch of text messages she had found on her husband's cellphone there had been one conversation that had devasted her:

I need to be able to vibe with someone when I'm with them.

Same here. It's not easy to vibe with someone, right?

It's not easy to vibe with someone, right? So many encounters in a single life. You can be with so many people, and yet there is one single person in the world who can capsize you.

So she got her cellphone out to send Vincent a message. It was like an SOS. She wanted to see him, speak to him, talk to him. About her life, her pathetic life.

***

At that very same moment, Vincent got his phone out to text Amélie. To tell her that love was fleeting and eternal, instantaneous and never-ending, spectacular and pathetic, miserly and generous, intense and insipid, tender and cruel. That it was truth and lies, passion and reason, honesty and hypocrisy, spontaneous and manipulative, gentle and brutal, a rise and fall, magnificent and miserable, joy and sadness, illusion and reality, hope and despair.

Tell her that you had to go from laughter to tears, from words to silence, from conversations to curses, from songs to screaming, from the profound to the superficial, from ecstasy to indifference, from jealousy to the desire to be rid of the other, from a dream to a nightmare, from desire to disgust, from pleasure to pain, from delight to horror, from fantasies about the other to fantasies of killing them, from idealism to fatalism, from the imaginary to the real, from soulmate to henchman, from lover to brother, then from brother to enemy, from mistress to mother then sister, from sister to cousin, from cousin to neighbor, from the wedding ceremony to court, from poems to insults, from speaking loving words to shouting, from shouting to lawyer's letters, from romanticism to cynicism, from action to submission, from awe to disappointment, from the surprising to the trivial, from losing track of time to feeling bored, from being unable to be alone to the vital need for independence, from the individual to the universal, from exclusivity to sharing, from trust to fear, from deference to condescension, from admiration to scorn, from kindness to destruction, from happiness to unhappiness, to despair. Or perhaps love was none of that. Perhaps none of that had anything to do with love. It wasn't about feelings, or a sensual encounter, or even a friendly one. It was a question of timing. He had crossed his wife's path at the moment she was emotionally available, the moment she dreamed of encountering love, the moment she wanted to have children. In a bid to turn the hackneyed concept of *kairos* into something much grander— the right moment that determines life which we neglect in the name of great ideals—we talk of love. Above all, he wanted to tell her that it is possible to love several times in life, but you only really have one love.

How are you Amélie?
  So-so, and you? she replied.
  Same here . . .
  Are you in Paris?
  No he wrote. *On vacation, with Sophie and the children.*
  Oh, nice. You take them on vacation.
  Not often enough, apparently! he answered.
  They complain? she asked.
  Oh they complain a lot.
  Oh, I'm sorry to hear that! she wrote back.

In fact, she was ecstatic. She hung on to those short sentences, those little nothings, those more or lesses. She told herself everything was still possible for them even now.

When are you coming back? she asked.

So he told her. He told her he had moved, that he had left Paris and was living in Hong Kong and developing his business, that he had decided to start a new life there, that he liked that life, even if it meant working a lot. He'd call her the next time he was back in Paris. He'd like to see her again.

She was dismayed by his tone. She was shocked he hadn't asked her opinion before leaving. She would have said no. No! *How could he do that to me?* she wondered. He hadn't even told her he was leaving. He hadn't thought about her—little her, her moods, her life, her pathetic boring existence, what she could or couldn't do. It didn't matter to him since he didn't love her!

Eyes wide open and eyelids twitching, she thought about how this small wound would hurt more than discovering her husband had had an affair and a child with another woman, and that, in fact, love didn't exist.

13.

It was pitch dark in the apartment. Sophie was asleep, alone in her bed. In the room beside her, Jules woke up. He had heard a noise, a door opening. He got up, trembling, and took care not to wake his sister as he silently slipped out of the room. The intruder walked down the hallway, went into the dining room, and opened the drawers, one by one, but didn't take the jewelry or money; he was looking for something else. Hidden, the child watched him, fear etched on his face.

Then the man found what he was looking for: photo albums. Using the flashlight function on his iPhone, he flicked through them: wedding photos, photos from vacations with the children, photos of everyday things. Only then did Jules recognize his father.

In the narrow beam of light, Vincent looked at the photos from his wedding day. He had changed so much. He had aged—his hair now salt and pepper, and the creases around his eyes were more marked, like his cheeks. He had lost weight over the past few months when he had lost his appetite. He had almost regained the figure he had when he was twenty.

But why had he let himself propose to her? He had thought he was in love with her, and surely he must have been, for a season, an hour, a minute perhaps. The magic of the moment no doubt—along with pressure from his family and the fact he had been brought up well. Because he was kind, nice. To please his parents and, above all, his father-in-law by whom he had been so impressed.

No, that wasn't the entire truth. He had been about to leave her, but then she had told him she was pregnant. An accident? Maybe, but at that point it no longer mattered if he wasn't in love. That was how he'd been brought up; that's what had been drummed into him, right from the start. Then he had put on weight, along with her. He worked a lot, read, didn't sleep, and lay awake all night in agony with an excruciating ulcer, forever anxious. He had suffered in silence for a long time. Suffered from the distance, the silence, the shouting, the unfairness of his life which wasn't his life, the alienation, the sorrow, the rage occasionally. He was suffering from the lack of love. He had tried his best to remain staunch, faithful to his promise, faithful to her too, but had lost his soul. With each day that passed, his very being was drained. He was downcast, aching, sad. His wife wasn't acting anymore, apart from at home where she performed *The Taming of the Shrew*. She stayed home, waiting, and becoming ever more bitter. She shouted constantly, screamed at him and at the children, gave him orders, and told him what to do, and he did it. She was always angry at the children. They were afraid of her, but not of him. It was as though their roles had been reversed. The best moments were the vacations, when he took his family to the station, not to go on vacation with them but to stay and work in Paris. They hadn't gone away together since the summer of the fatal revelation, but he had started to travel. He had just returned from a work trip to New York; he often went to London, where he had moved after Hong Kong. This time, when he had landed, he hadn't been able to bring himself to set foot in his home again. He had gone to a hotel, set down his cases along with his heavy heart, and then gone to his apartment in the middle of the night to get his belongings and the photo albums before leaving.

Vincent looked up; his eyes met his Jules's. His son had understood. Vincent hugged him for a few minutes, struggling to hold back his tears. Then, afraid Sophie would wake up and make a scene, he hurried away to give his sleeping daughter a quick kiss. He filled a bag with a few of his things, the photo albums, and a book, just one book from the bookcase, from his past, from one specific day that had remained etched on his memory even though he didn't really know why, a book containing a name and telephone number. And then he left his own home without making a single sound, like a burglar.

The next day, he left Sophie a message, caught the train to Paris, and arrived in the evening. His cellphone buzzed with insults, pleas, and threats, so he blocked her.

How can you break up without abandoning your own convictions? And bring closure to a relationship that had lasted so long? How could he understand it all and admit he was wrong? That he hadn't believed in their relationship for a long time, that he'd had the first child without really wanting to and the second one out of duty. How do you explain that to yourself? Or simply explain it? How was he going to undo everything he had built up with his father-in-law, that flourishing company? And face the uncertainty of the future? With attacks and rising terrorism in cities heightening the sense of risk. He was sitting in a bar in Rue du Bac, not far from where he used to live. People around him were drinking, talking, laughing. His iPhone lay on the table beside him, and he wondered who he could meet that evening. The world was within easy reach, but he didn't have any friends left. With his traveling, and after he got married, they had all gradually grown apart. His parents were elderly, and he didn't want to worry them by confiding in them or having to give explanations. He had even lost contact with Charles, his best friend. His wife had kept his parents, family, and friends at a distance. They lived in a vacuum, isolated from the rest of the world. He was alone. He drank a beer, then a second one, then a third, and out of the blue, he felt a sense of urgency. On the outside, he appeared perfectly calm, cool, and collected, but deep down there was a sense of contained elation. He checked his Facebook account, then his Instagram. And then he saw her. Amélie, a story showing her hosting a writer in her bookstore. Amélie, photos, black and white, elegant, understated. And Paris, the setting sun, the rain, a rainbow, winter. Her bookstore with light wooden bookshelves. At a book fair. In summer, at the seaside. In winter, in a ski suit. At a cocktail party, a dinner, a concert. A smile on her face, looking youthful, smooth. And her comments—sensitive, melancholic, ever more philosophical, about life, love, writing. Quoting Albert Cohen, Rilke. Amélie, true to herself. And Amélie, always alone in the photos.

He felt his heart pound and followed her account. A few minutes later, she followed him back. He sent her a message on Instagram.

Parisian?

Parisian for a day, Parisian always. And you? she wrote.

I came back.

For good? she asked.

This time, yes. Too late for a drink? he asked.

No, but I have to get up really early, for the children.

So we've got a few hours . . . he replied.

So? Either I pull on my PJs, or I set an alarm.

Or perhaps both. But why PJs?

Because I've just had a bath and I don't feel like getting dressed.

Ah, okay . . . goodnight then, Amélie!

But who said you can't go for a drink in your PJs?

True, who said that? she replied.

You, I believe.

Me?

I'll pull on my PJs and then we can meet, she answered.

Where? he asked.

At the Eiffel Tower? she suggested.

Okay.

Are you serious?

Why wouldn't I be?

10 minutes, at the Eiffel Tower, she confirmed.

That evening, the Eiffel Tower was surprised to see them reunited below it. She felt good in her skin and was glowing, radiant with joy and enthusiasm. She had never looked so good, different, relaxed, cheerful, and as happy as a lark as Prévert would say, even though larks aren't happy. They're neither happy nor sad because there is a time for everything.

He asked her how she was, what she was doing, and how the bookstore was going. It had been hard since Amazon; people had started buying books online. She didn't know what the future had in store. She had been on her own with the children since her divorce. On her own? That surprised him and threw him off balance. So he asked how she was, really. What stage she was at. *He wanted to know.* But what exactly? Was she available? Was she in a relationship?

Then, in the middle of a sentence, he stopped listening to the words she was saying—he wanted her. He felt light-headed as joy and sadness swirled deep within him. He delighted in her company; he was overjoyed to see her again. He wanted to talk to her, tell her so many things, show her how strong his feelings were, take her in his arms, embrace her, and hold her all night for the rest of his life.

So without having heard a word she had said, he told her he loved her, that he had loved her since that first shy glance, first silence, first half kiss, first goodbye, first missed date, first call she didn't pick up, first misunderstanding, first gap, first marriage, first child, first divorce. He admired her so much, yet she seemed so far beyond his reach that simply touching her felt impossible. Hadn't they known each other for twenty years? Twenty years of silenced love, twenty years of distance that only ended when his hand brushed against hers. Twenty years of glances, lunches, talking about anything and everything yet leaving things left unsaid. Twenty years of desire that suddenly exploded like a thousand rivers flowing into an ocean. All that distance was suddenly swept away. He wanted to cry, laugh, rejoice, look at her, live from her, through her, in her, and via her, eat and drink her instead of eating and drinking in front of her, and, in awe, watch her live.

It was a solemn moment. She had waited her entire life to hear those words, but she didn't try to comprehend it. She wasn't listening, wasn't looking, and didn't understand. Her love for him was alive, as alive as it had been every day for the past twenty years. It had grown, trembled, quivered, fret, lit up or died down, sighed, and been annoyed, impatient, hungry, thirsty—it wasn't dead, but it had been thrown off course, disillusioned even.

Then, the twinkling lights of the Eiffel Tower went out, and she slipped away in the dark. In sneakers and PJs, she ran as fast as she could until she was out of breath and her heart pounded.

14.

After the Eiffel Tower, the confession, the emotions, and a run through the night, Amélie arrived home exhausted. Those words, that long-awaited gesture—she didn't understand why it had all happened at that moment in time, that evening, that instant. Overcome by a wave of dizziness, she lay down fully dressed and fell asleep, thoroughly perplexed and astonished.

A few months earlier, she had met Jérémie in the Café Charbon, a Parisian bistro in Rue Oberkampf with a typical steel bar and a thousand bottles hanging on the wall behind it.

He had been waiting for her, sitting in a dark, blood-red, maroon booth seat: a handsome man with brown hair, dark eyes, glowing olive-toned skin, a charming smile, and a straight back.

"Hello Amélie. I'm glad to see it's you. I noticed you as soon as you walked in. I was thinking . . . I hope she's that girl I met on the Meetic app!"

In a few seconds, they had shared the essentials. She was divorced; he was single, younger than her. They wanted to get to know each other.

She had been on her own since the divorce—broke and forced to start again from scratch. In an agreement she had reached with her ex-husband's lawyer, she had given up everything to get custody of the children. Fabrice had been even more ruthless during the divorce proceedings than during their marriage. He had taken everything, including the apartment she had bought with her own savings. All she had left was her bookstore and books that were getting harder and harder to sell. She had lost everything she had built up over those long years. It had all collapsed like a house of cards, both love and, by extension her own ideals, on the day she had discovered her husband had another daughter whom he had abandoned.

When she was feeling lonely one evening while the children were at their father's, she had followed Clara's advice had signed up on an online dating site. She had immediately discovered a selection of characters and personalities, people to be played like cards. Profile photos with faces or sometimes backs, head-to-toe shots, or portraits: men, men, and more men. So many possibilities just a few feet away, just one click away on her computer. So much hope in those doldrums of loneliness and despair!

When she had entered that café in Rue Oberkampf, it had been her first ever date. They had a drink, then another, and another. It got late, and he offered her a lift, the most natural thing in the world, like they had been lovers forever. They kissed in the car, then on her doorstep, and she settled into his embrace like it was something she did every evening, so they could get to know each other, see each other. She knew Meetic made it easy to date, quick and straightforward, no strings. But he had called her the next day, wanting to see her that evening. She said she couldn't—she was afraid. She was protecting herself because she had already suffered too much, but he insisted. When she hung up, she felt happy, swept up in being desired and wanted. They didn't know what to say when they met again in the same café. She looked at him. He was attractive with his charmingly arched eyes and thin mouth. He took her hand, but she pulled it away. He wanted to kiss her in the car again, and she let him.

So he sent her a few more text messages. She canceled their dates—she thought they weren't a good match, that he was too young, and told him they should stop texting each other. *I'm in the process of missing out on something beautiful*, she thought. *Something great, but I can't do this, I'm no longer capable of loving someone.* A few days passed, sad and gloomy. Then one evening she went out with old friends from her student days near the Bastille. Some of them she had stayed in touch with, and others she had found again through Facebook. Now forty-five, Clara's love life had been as turbulent as her career. The others had gotten married and had children, then got divorced. They had all remarried and had more children with other people, or not. They were all broken, starting over, damaged, and crushed by life.

Jérémie appeared in the middle of the group, daunted yet happy, and when he leaned over to kiss Amélie she felt her heart pound. So they had held their own secret conversation in parallel to the general conversation, a conversation to which only they held the keys.

"When my wedding day came around, I didn't want to go through with it," she said. "My father was the one who took me by the hand and told me to go on."

"Why didn't you want to go through with it?" he asked.

"I thought I was making a huge mistake," she replied.

"So why did you?"

"Because I was in love with someone else who was in love with someone else."

And that someone else, she thought, *had left without even saying goodbye. That someone else must have forgotten me by now. He's becoming fainter in my mind too, like a distant memory. I hardly think about him now. He's no longer on my mind the way he once was.* That someone else had children with someone else, so he didn't love her. And that thought suddenly freed her heart and left her free to love.

As they left the café, they held hands, and like the first time they had met, she ended up in his arms in his car. Suddenly everything changed on the banks of the Seine lit up by the Eiffel Tower's familiar lights twinkling in the night.

A new life began for Amélie: she would make dinner for the children, put them to bed, jump in the bath, get dressed, put on some makeup, go out, meet him, kiss, embrace, then dash home before dawn. They got to know each other. Her: her parents, her degree, her bookstore, her divorce, and her children who were her entire world. Him: his childhood in a neighborhood on the outskirts of the city, his father's small restaurant, his family, his detached house, his garden, and his job as a car salesman.

One evening, he invited her to the restaurant they both liked, the bistro in Rue Oberkampf that had become their lucky talisman.

"I have a confession to make," he said.

"What?" she asked.

"Well, it's hard to put it into words, but you must know already. I'm not cultured. I haven't read a single thing in my life, I didn't even graduate from high school. You use a lot of words I don't understand. You need to know. I don't want you to get the wrong impression about me."

That was the moment she realized she was in love. The woman who had thought her heart had wizened, that love was dead and buried. The woman who had been freed after having been locked up in that prison created around her by society, her family, and fairy tales. The woman who thought she had returned from everything she had lived through, her marriage, her children, and falling out of love with her husband who no longer loved her. She felt like she had been born anew in this man's eyes. She made peace with herself, with love, and the celebration of life.

They didn't have an address; they had places: his car,

the banks of the Seine, restaurants, her apartment, every neighborhood, and every street. They didn't have their own address, but Paris belonged to them. The lights along the Seine were theirs when she came home late and her children were asleep. The secret gardens where they had picnics on their dates in spring. The Eiffel Tower when the city was deserted in the month of August. The Marais and its cobblestones that glistened on rainy autumn days, and the Ile Saint-Louis decorated like a postcard. The Trocadero, which offered its spectacular view of the Eiffel Tower in the cold of winter. Paris had changed and become that fantastical, phantasmatic, intense, and unreal city.

And so she had forgotten Vincent. Until he had contacted her to arrange that unlikely encounter under the Eiffel Tower. So she had fled, running as fast as she could toward the man she loved, the man who inhabited her nights and days, and above all toward her new life—because she was pregnant.

15.

After their encounter under the Eiffel Tower, Vincent walked for a long time through the night. He wondered why Amélie had fled: it must have been because of him, obviously. She didn't love him and wasn't attracted to him; he had just imagined she was available when perhaps she wasn't.

He had been wrong. He had been unable to see clearly in this curious game of life, love, and luck. He had been wrong about his own feelings for so long, and now he had declared his love for a woman who didn't want him. A life together—it wasn't to be. Not for him, not for her. He thought he had fled her when she had been fleeing him!

It was the middle of the night, and it wasn't long before he arrived at Place de la Sorbonne where they had first met. It felt like yesterday even though it had been more than twenty years ago. He had waited for her and she hadn't turned up. It had been a sign, fate. Yet they had caught each other's eye waiting in that line in the hallway. He remembered how strongly he had been attracted to her, so young, childlike, innocent, and unaccomplished, just starting out in life. He remembered their first conversation, their smiles, that night they had spent talking about everything and nothing, about love too. It suddenly struck him that that had been the night he had fallen in love without realizing it. Love at first sight that would never fade, that would last. He had told her she was beautiful, and everything could have changed in that instant. He had wanted to take her hand and kiss her. He should have remained silent, but instead he had kept talking and kept the conversation going. He hadn't had the courage; he had thought he would have time, later. When they had left at four in the morning, there had been a moment of hesitation, of course. He had wanted to take her back to his place, had almost suggested it, then had second thoughts and told himself it was too soon and he didn't want it to go too fast. So she had left in a taxi and given him a little wave goodbye, and he had walked home, happy and light, like he was suddenly full of joy. A feeling he'd never really experienced again, until now, when he realized she was the one. What had happened during all that time? Had an evil god or a nervy genie slipped into their relationship to take him at his word and inflict a cruel punishment on him?

The square was empty, silent. A man lay asleep on the street. He too had left his home, carrying only a suitcase. Vincent could lie down beside that poor wretch, too. He was free and lost. He didn't know where to go, so he began to roam the streets. There was grey Paris, romantic Paris, nostalgic Paris, and dreary Paris. Adventurous Paris along the docks on the banks of the 13th arrondissement. Too much gray Paris with rainy, long-drawn-out Sundays when all the shutters were down and there was nothing to do. Paris in April when everything reemerged and came back to life. Paris in the snow when the traffic halted and cars crept along, afraid of skidding. Paris in the summer when the streets emptied and the shops shut, when the bakeries, fishmongers, and even the bookstores closed. One August 15th he had spent the public holiday entirely alone while his wife was away on vacation with the children. Not a single sound in the entire neighborhood. Not a single shop or bakery open, a ghost town. He had walked along the banks of the Seine with a strange sense of freedom and solitude, anguish, and fulfillment. There had been parties, happy nights, sad nights, wandering nights, then sleepless nights. There had been Gainsbourg songs in the early hours. Smoky bars, smiles, and laughter. Paris when he had studied under the green lamps in the Saint-Geneviève library, the temple of the second-year literature students. Paris that screamed poverty, that was hungry and often cold. The Paris of hidden resources, sumptuous residences, private mansions, and huge terraces.

The Paris of doors banging and windows rattling in storms. Cold Paris teeming with crowds on New Year's Eve. He dreamed of gay Paris of Montparnasse in the roaring twenties, when artists lived, sang, and danced together, drew, wrote, and partied until dawn. Giddy after a night out, he loved crossing the Seine on his way home and looking at the Eiffel Tower through the windows of a cab on a summer night. Soaking up the twilight on a terrace, people-watching. Scorching hot summers or cold rainy ones caused by climate change. Fall seasons that still had a hint of summer. The spring times that never arrived. He no longer knew when winter began or when the seasons changed. He had lost his bearings. The deafening existential crisis was in the process of revealing itself. Now in middle age, he wondered what his life was worth without love.

16.

"But Madame, what happened? Why has your income dropped so drastically over the past three years?"

"People have stopped buying books. They don't read anymore. Not on the bus, or the train, or in waiting rooms. Some doctors have dispensed with magazines entirely because no one reads them. No one reads before they go to bed either. Even I don't read anymore! The TV shows about culture have all disappeared too, apart from *La Grande Librairie*. But no one watches it because they've stopped reading. So I'm not selling anything at all! Nowadays, few books sell more than 500 copies."

"It's that bad?"

"Everyone's on their cellphones, just like you and me. Social networks, Facebook, Instagram, Tinder. That's all everyone does now! And that's not even the worst of it. The worst of all is Netflix. Netflix has killed us off. Everyone's hooked on their favorite series."

"You're right, that's all I watch—series. Have you seen *You*? It's excellent."

"I prefer *The Spy*."

"Oh, is it good?"

"Yes, gripping."

"What did you think of the last season of *House of Cards*?"

"It wasn't great. I preferred *Scandal*."

"Well then, what do you plan to do?"

"I don't know. What do you suggest?"

"You need to reduce your outgoings. You do realize you can't continue like this, right?"

"I've already considered that. I'm making cuts. I only buy clothes at discount stores. I've moved to a smaller apartment. I take the metro and the bus. I can't do any more than that."

"If you can't reduce your outgoings further, you'll have to find a way to increase your income."

"Which one? I've got a bookstore, remember. What exactly would you like me to do?"

"Please don't adopt that tone with me, Madame. I'm just trying to tell you that the bank will no longer be able to serve you . . ."

"No longer be able to serve me? But don't you realize I've had an account with you for fifteen years? I'm a loyal customer, with highs and lows of course, but loyal all the same, and I've had good years. You know that better than anyone."

"But not since your divorce. We're going through a financial and economic crisis that is affecting every-one, Madame, and your income is clearly not enough to support your current lifestyle, no more than your book-store can. We can't wipe out your debts. We're a bank you understand, not a credit agency. Couldn't you sell other books? Ones that work. Bestsellers?"

"I sell those too," says Amélie. "And paper, pens, post-cards, and even jewelry! I've turned my bookstore into a concept store. I wouldn't be able to keep it open otherwise."

"Excellent idea!"

"Unfortunately it's not enough. Listen, I've got a per-sonal relationship with my banker, and I would like to stay with this bank if possible."

"I know . . . I'm sorry, but you've been in the red for two years now and . . . well, I have to tell you that our bank's policy has changed, and we've considered guiding you toward . . ."

"Toward where?"

"Well, toward the exit. Am I being clear?"

"Extremely clear. How long have I got before I have to close the shop?"

"Until December 31st this year, Madame."

Penniless and child-free, Amélie returned to her tiny apartment in the Marais. Her bookstore was on the verge of bankruptcy. Her ex-husband had managed to get joint custody of the children by turning them against her and exerting a huge amount of control over them, so much so that they had even testified against their own mother. Fa-brice still texted her every day, despite having abandoned his mistress and daughter to start another family with a woman who had three children of her own. They made the perfect family, a family her own children were now part of, as testified by the "Happy Family" WhatsApp group her ex-husband had created. The Happy Family drove a 4×4, lived in Neuilly, and went on vacation to the other side of the world, yet left its children without adult supervision, allowed them to binge-watch Netflix series, play video games, and vape, and never took any interest in their homework or how much they slept. The children would arrive at her place starving, exhausted, and aggressive. Forced to count out odd and even weeks and the days that didn't count, they never got more than 2 out of 20 in math. Two weeks, two children, two households. Everything in their lives involved a two. Even their phone numbers were full of twos. They had two of everything: school things, clothes, birthdays, and families. No need for glasses, they had two houses where they forgot everything: their exercise books, their homework, their friends, their ideas, their dreams, their desires, their future, their past, and even who they were. One week they were on Instagram, Facebook, and WhatsApp until three in the morning, and the next they worked. One week they played Fortnite, and the next they played piano. One week they got 18 out of 20 in French, the next they got 2. Poor divided bodies that hadn't asked for any of that. Poor little hearts cut in two. They hadn't wanted their parents to separate or to pay the price for it. They hadn't wanted equality. All they had wanted was for the battle to end. The battle for the children, the battle between husband

and wife, the disaster they had seen sweep into their daily lives. Watching them grow up was so painful and so wonderful at the same time that Amélie occasionally dreamed of abandoning everything and heading off to the other side of the world with them, gone for good.

As for her, she was half a woman, part father, part mother, part bookseller, part teacher, part nanny, and part cook. One week was spent on homework, school, mealtimes, games, and the family, and the next she was free. Thanks to equality, she had also regained liberty. Fraternity too, since she now had time to see her friends again.

For the past three years, she had grieved for the child that should have been born yet died in her womb. That thing that is never mentioned, that doesn't exist, yet is nonetheless present, carrying all of one's dreams. The baby that did not arrive, the dead fetus, the failed dream, Jérémie's child, the one she had desired so much no longer existed, would never exist, apart from in her memories. Sometimes a girl, sometimes a boy, the imaginary baby had all kinds of faces, every face possible, and she loved it with a love that was both imaginary and real.

Jérémie had left her when she had told him she was pregnant. He thought she had trapped him, he didn't want a child, and he felt he was too young and not ready yet, he had said. Did he know she had lost the baby? She didn't know. He hadn't been back to see her. She often wondered if he had abandoned her with his child, like her husband had left his mistress and daughter, that little girl who looked so much like him. Deep down, that question

114

tormented her. How could you reject your own child? Because of the circumstances, fear, cowardice, indifference, cruelty. . .

She was a mother to the child she had lost through miscarriage and mother to the half-children she had half the time, victims of their father's manipulation. She was hosting strangers from time to time and had a child buried in her head. All those imaginary sons and daughters, loved with a real love. That was how it was. One day, she had had whole children, the next, she had none. One day, she had been in love, then she wasn't. She had wept so much that her heart had wisened.

After the appointment at the bank, she passed the mother of one of her students, walking down the street with her three children. When the woman saw her, she lowered her gaze, embarrassed. This woman, whom she didn't know, had seen fit to give testimony against her. Lies and hypocrisy, vanity and jealousy . . .

She went home, had a bath, and got ready to go out for dinner. She looked at herself in the mirror. Now over fifty, the wrinkles on her forehead and around her eyes were deepening, more mature, clearer. Her face, like her body, carried the mark of time against which she battled as best she could to appear young, fasting and exercising . . . She had cut her hair and dressed modestly in jeans, a white sweater, and sneakers.

Her friend Clara had invited her and a few other old friends for a reunion, roommates from their student days with whom they had lost touch. They had used an on-line meeting scheduling tool to set the date a long time ago. Amélie didn't really feel like going, but she couldn't get out of it. She didn't believe in any of it anymore, not in love, or playing along with society, or friendship and friends from the past. She didn't know what the next day would bring. She was tired and wondered what the meaning of her life was, the meaning of life in general. When she visited her elderly parents in Bernay, she redis-covered the tranquility of the countryside. It calmed her bruised soul, and she thought that perhaps it wasn't the worst place in the world. Her parents had softened with age and had become kinder. By making peace with them, she made peace with herself, with her childhood. They had been together for sixty years. They had gotten used to each other. Had they been right? Had they been wrong?

She caught an Uber across Paris and marveled at the street names: Rue Rosa-Bonheur, Rue Dieu, Rue Sainte-Félicité . . . She loved the broad, straight avenues in the 8th arrondissement, the medieval streets, the squares, Place la Bastille, Place de la Republique, and even Place de la Nation. Moving from one arrondissement to the next was like a journey through the changing urban and social landscape. She had loved every neighborhood she had lived in, fell into routines there, made friends, and found her bearings, along with the local greengrocer, markets, and gyms.

She loved Paris for the creepers and lampposts, the

streets leading up the hill, and the ones leading down-hill, the dilapidated houses, the social housing and the upmarket neighborhoods, the tiny maids' rooms with a toilet in the hallway, the never-ending apartments, the riverbanks, the evening lights, the nights, the early mornings after sleepless nights, the dark or pale dawns, the birds that sang, the pigeons on the cobblestones, the sad parks in the winter, and the Jardin du Luxembourg, the majestic Place Vendôme, the bridges, the nighttime, the riverbanks, the eternal mailmen even though there are no longer any letters, the museums, the traffic jams, the lovers embracing, and those images by Épinal. She loved it for the promises and caresses, the busy Saturdays, and sad Sundays, the things that remain unresolved when doors close. She loved it because it doesn't give itself up easily and is instantly elusive. She loved it for everything said and left unsaid, what she lived and did not live, for that unfathomable melancholy, that attachment to the past and nostalgia, for that daydream that grips you when you see it—Paris.

Finally, there they all were, happy to be reunited in Clara's apartment, listening to Massive Attack, reminiscing about their past, the huge parties, the other roommates they had had too, like that Swiss German, or perhaps he'd been Croatian, who had stayed for three months and no one had known who he was, where he went, or what his name was. And the visit from Amélie's parents who had thought each room had its own bathroom. And how their time together had come to an end when a gas leak had turned the apartment into a deathtrap and they'd had to leave the windows open and wear winter jackets and hats during the cold winter. They could have died, asphyxiated one night and been found dead the next morning. They wouldn't have gotten married, would never have loved, never gotten divorced, never won or lost—and it wouldn't have turned out any worse. In the middle of the buzzing conversation, one snippet made Amélie jump. Someone quietly asked: *Have you heard from Vincent Brunel?* And another replied, *I heard about him via a friend. He left his wife and is back in Paris. On his own? On his own.*

The world suddenly started to spin around Amélie and she felt dizzy.

She got up from the table, took her phone and, hands shaking, wrote to Vincent to ask him what he was doing. Her heart skipped a beat when he immediately replied, *Waiting for you.*

17.

On May 20, 2018, Amélie arrived at the café on Place de la Sorbonne to find Vincent sitting on the terrace. She paused to look at him. His hair was longer around his face, and he hadn't shaved for several days. Dressed in jeans and a blue shirt, his boyish figure transported her back thirty years, back to that same square at the Sorbonne. He took out a watch—an old pocket watch—and checked the time, looked around, worried, and then he saw her.

When she sat down opposite him, he didn't say a word. He studied her face in silence. They looked at each other for a while. With their wrinkles, gray hair, and tired eyes suggesting a sleepless night—that attraction from their youth was still there, like the first time they had met, returning after a very, very long journey.

Thirty years earlier, they had been young and carefree. Encounters, love, life, work, parents, children . . . none of that had really mattered. And then, in the small hours over a drink in the Café des Capucines, they had talked until dawn, barely whispering.

"*Do you believe in it?*"

"*Of course I believe in it.*"

"*True love?*"

"*That too. And you?*"

They hadn't understood. They hadn't dared. They had both been trapped by their upbringing, their inhibitions; they didn't know. They were unaware that life gets the better of encounters like that, and love; that you gradually get carried along despite yourself, caught up by a fate you no longer control; that you choose forks in the road, or doors into hallways, hallways that last ten, twenty, thirty years; that you often marry the person you don't love; that you let the love of your life go, out of fragility, or bad luck, or inadvertently; that you don't have children with the person you love, and then those children are the reason you stay with that person, and also the reason you end up separating.

"Wonderful to see you again, Amélie," he murmured. "Thanks for getting in touch . . . So how have you been?"

"It's a long story. How about you? Tell me about you . . ."

"I've been shuttling back and forth to London to see the children since the divorce. It's not easy. But I do my best for them, for me, for us," he said.

"How old are they?" she asked.

"Jules is fifteen, and Joséphine is ten."

Neither of them spoke.

"And yours?" he asked.

"Arthur is twelve and Pauline is ten too."

"They're still young."

"Yes, too young to deal with everything we're putting them through. Sometimes I think I should have just accepted it—to spare them all of that," she replied.

"It takes a lot of courage to divorce," he added.

"It did indeed."

They looked at each other and smiled. Then he gently took her hand, that hand he had hesitated to touch thirty years earlier, and which, for the first time, she let rest in his.

"And your work?" she asked.

"Oh that . . . I gave it all up. I was working with my father-in-law, you know. I lost everything in the divorce. I actually had to leave the company," he explained.

"We pay a high price for our mistakes, don't we?"

"Yes, a very high price indeed," he agreed.

"What are you doing now?" she asked.

"Music."

"Can you make a living from it?"

"No. Everything's so different now. It's all on platforms, and there's a lot of new technology. I play at concerts, but it's not enough. Thankfully I've got a few ideas and a bit of know-how. At least I won't have worked for nothing. And what about you? Tell me about you . . ." he asked.

"Well," she said, "I hate not seeing my children every day, and I hate seeing how much like him they are, copying his expressions, resembling him. When they're with me, I feel like I'm looking at him, his double. It all feels so absurd."

"So you didn't love your husband?" he asked.

"Well, I guess I did love him—for a summer. What about you, your wife?"

"The first few years were great. Then it changed after the children were born. No, perhaps before that. Perhaps I never loved her at all. I was young when I met her," he replied.

"Not as young as when we met," she said.

"Why didn't you show up for our date here? I waited for you, you know. Perhaps it was all just a dream, and you've only just arrived now? Maybe I've spent thirty years waiting for you in this café. I knew you'd turn up— one day."

"I did come," she replied.

"You came," he said, his face lighting up. "Thirty years late. That's extremely late indeed!"

"So you really did like me?" she asked.

"Yes. I liked you. And what about you?"

"Oh yes . . . but I was too shy."

"But why . . . why didn't you say that sooner?"

"I'd been taught to never make the first move, never take the initiative, never say what I thought, to stay quiet and listen, to stay in the background. I thought the date had been a misunderstanding, a coincidence. Or that maybe you needed new glasses. Or you'd just feel obliged to turn up, after our first encounter," she explained.

"Do you remember how we talked all night? That had

never happened to me before. I think I was crazy. Crazy about you . . ."

Her hand was still resting in his. He stroked her cheek.

"Me too," she said.

"Well then, what happened that day? Why were you late?"

"I couldn't."

"Couldn't what?"

"I was so ugly!"

"Ugly?"

"Back then, I was really ugly. Don't you remember? My bangs, my clothes . . ." she continued.

"I remember calling you. You didn't pick up. I also remember that you were stunning. Not quite as stunning as you are now though," he told her.

"I did pick up the phone that day, but I was too late. There was no one on the other end of the line. So I quickly got dressed, I got ready to go out, but . . ."

It wasn't a date she had missed that day—it had been her entire life.

"When we saw each other again ten years later," she continued, "you were married."

"I'd met Sophie. I thought she was the love of my life."

"I realized you didn't love her when you told me you had discovered what love really meant when your children were born."

"Why?" he asked.

"It meant you didn't love your wife," she replied.

"Yes, that's true," he smiled. "Life is so strange: you have children with someone you wouldn't even be friends with. Just because they crossed your path at the right moment in time. The right moment is enough for two people to meet, get together, and have children even though they don't have anything in common. And the wrong moment in time is enough for other people to fail to come together when in fact everything brings them together . . ."

It seemed that finally, after all this time, they were laying down arms and starting the conversation they should have had thirty years earlier. *How are you? What's your life like? Who are you? How do you feel? What do you desire? What do you want, from the start? It's a long story, I'll have to tell you. We have all the time in the world. No, we don't have all the time in the world. Life has been rough on us. We've lost a lot of time; we must tell each other everything.*

Their eyes searched for the other's and met—two souls hungry for each other. She was amazed, surprised almost, that she felt so captivated. It was like she was seeing him for the first time. She examined her heart. Her desire was so strong she thought she'd be burned if she even touched him.

They had known each other for thirty years. Thirty years to learn how to talk to each other, to tell each other the truth. Marriages, divorces, bereavements, children, hundreds of trips, sometimes to the other side of the world, successes, failures, pain, hopes, disappointments, lost childhood dreams, ruined childhoods.

She had done everything she could to forget him—

throughout her entire life. So much absence and solitude, so much anguish, so much heaviness. And that feeling of waiting, breathless, that permanent tension that only ever eased when she saw him. The years when they had lost touch had been years of unspoken love that only ended when he looked at her again that night, on that square, and thirty years of dreams and desire exploded like a thousand rivers into an ocean as the walls separating them were broken down as his arm brushed against her and it wasn't by accident. The simple gesture gave rise to a sense of happiness within her that surpassed everything else, and which, for the first time in her life, made her feel like she truly existed.

So he told her he had fallen in love with her the very first time he had seen her, and once more at that New Year's Eve party ten years later when they had seen each other again, but he wasn't alone. He had thought about her so often, but never dared tell her. Then life happened . . . Yes, we pay a high price for our mistakes, a very high price. He would never have believed she could want him. He didn't think he had a chance. He wouldn't have allowed himself to picture it. Picture what?

That they could still love.

And love each other.

She asked him why their love was impossible, and he replied that the thing that was impossible was knowing to what extent it was possible.

They fell silent and looked at each other as they had

never dared to before, a fiery passion in their eyes, and then the server arrived with the menu.

"What would you like?"